Death on the Page

Revenge on the Reviewer

A Murder Mystery

I0629869

By Tom McAuliffe

NEXT STOP PARADISE
PUBLISHING
Ft. Walton Beach, Florida, USA

Death on the Page
Revenge on the Reviewer

Printed in the United States of America.
First Edition - 2025

For more information, email:
BookInfo@nextstopparadise.com

Please visit:
www.authortommcauliffe.com

<u>Dedication</u>

To the Men and Women of
Law enforcement, especially the pros of
crime scene investigations.

To the LEOs (Law Enforcement Officers)
in my family: Sgt. Jerry Hunter and
Officer Eric Harpe and my friend
and adviser Detective Mark Lapinski

TABLE OF CONTENTS

PROLOGUE

Ethan Cole is a man who wears ambition like a second skin, his every step, word, and gesture betraying an Intense, almost obsessive desire for validation. In his early forties, Ethan looks like someone who has spent too many years alone with his thoughts. His face is sharp and angular, with high cheekbones and hollowed eyes suggesting constant internal unrest. A few gray streaks in his dark hair, gave him an air of intellectual gravity that complements his tailored, slightly rumpled clothing —a carefully crafted look of the tortured artist.

Standing shy of six feet, he moves with a slight hesitancy as though perpetually distracted by thoughts no one else can follow. His slender frame and the slight stoop to his posture add to the impression of a man more comfortable hunched over a desk than mingling in public. He has pale, almost translucent skin, a mark of too many hours indoors writing, and a faint scar under his left eye—a remnant from a youthful accident he rarely speaks about, as if the scar itself was another piece of his carefully guarded identity.

Ethan's most defining feature, though, is his eyes. Blue and intense, they tend to fixate and linger too long, creating a slight discomfort in those under his gaze. His eyes miss nothing, always evaluating, dissecting, and analyzing people and their motives as though they were characters in one of his novels.

He doesn't speak much, but when he does, it's with the confidence of someone used to being listened to, his words clipped, occasionally sarcastic, with an edge that hints at frustration.

A sometimes-celebrated author, Ethan's drive for perfection is nearly pathological. Over the years, he has alienated friends, wives, lovers, and even colleagues with his uncompromising standards, but he brushes off the isolation as the price of 'genius.' His success has brought him a cult following; his fans are fiercely loyal. Yet, for Ethan, it's never enough. He craves the acknowledgment of the critics who dismiss him as a commercial writer, knowing that with each new novel, his respectability in literary circles hangs by a thread.

Underneath his aloof demeanor lies a well of insecurity he buries under arrogance and a biting wit. Ethan is deeply haunted by the idea that he's not the writer he believes he should be. Every word of criticism cuts him deeply, but he masks the hurt with a calm, calculating exterior. A determination to 'get even' starts to grow. And as the distance between his public persona and private self grows, so does the darkness festering within him—a darkness that pushes him to rationalize the unthinkable.

In many ways, Ethan sees himself as a tragic figure, a man misunderstood and underestimated, burdened by the curse of his intelligence and artistry. It is this belief, this sense of intellectual superiority, and wounded pride that makes him capable of crossing lines most people wouldn't dare approach. Ethan doesn't just want success; he wants a poetic justice that will leave the world recognizing his genius, no matter the cost.

For every yin, there's a yang... for every this, there's a that, and for Author Ethan Cole, there is Reviewer and critic Calvin Reese. Both emotional hemophiliacs, each needs the other.

A man who wields words like weapons, Reese is renowned for his unflinching and often brutal critiques of the literary world. In his mid-fifties, he has the bearing of someone who has seen—and judged—it all. His silver hair kept short and meticulously styled, adds to his commanding presence, and his piercing blue eyes make people feel uncomfortably scrutinized. Calvin's well-lined face still carries the sharp angles and high cheekbones of his youth, a face that somehow looks more dignified with age. He seems almost regal to those who meet him, moving through spaces as though he owns them, whether it's a crowded book signing, an intimate literary event, or one-on-one.

Physically, Reese is a lean, wiry man. His build reflects years of discipline that carry into every aspect of his life. His movements are precise and deliberate, each gesture calculated. His clothing—a rotation of well-tailored custom suits in dark tones —is as sharp as his reviews, chosen to project a professional detachment. It does. Though not particularly tall, he has an imposing aura that seems to expand well beyond his physical frame, commanding attention even in silence.

What truly defines Reese is his unshakeable sense of self-worth, bordering on arrogance. He's a critic who has earned his reputation through years of unapologetically harsh but undeniably insightful reviews. In the literary world, he's a kingmaker—or a king-breaker—his opinions holding sway over readers, publishers, and even authors themselves. Reese has developed a taste for the power his reviews wield; he knows that a single piece from him can elevate or ruin a career, and he revels in that authority. It's a job he considers almost sacred, seeing himself as a gatekeeper to quality literature, someone tasked with protecting readers from mediocrity.

This position, however, has made him something of a loner. His critiques have cost him friendships over the years, and he remains guarded, socially and emotionally, keeping colleagues and acquaintances at arm's length. Though respected, he's rarely liked and accepts this as the inevitable price of his honesty. Reese believes that the world would be a better place if more people spoke the truth, however cutting, and he is quick to dismiss anyone who views him as cruel or vindictive.

Yet, there's a thrill Reese gets from his role that he wouldn't admit to anyone, a secret delight in seeing the reactions his reviews provoke. It's not just about protecting literature, after all—it's about leaving a mark, shaping the discourse, and knowing that his words, unlike most, have the power to endure. Underneath his professional detachment, he savors his significance, seeing himself as an arbiter of taste, a man with a rare vision and a responsibility to elevate the art form.

For Reese, writers like Ethan Cole—commercially successful but artistically "inferior"—are precisely the sort he believes need humbling. To him, Ethan's latest novel wasn't just bad; it's emblematic of everything wrong with modern independent publishing, a symbol of how artistry is being sacrificed for sales. And Reese has no qualms about being the one to say it. Over the years, the hate between the two grew and became all-encompassing for both men, and it was pretty obvious that it all would not end well. To outsiders, the emotions stirred within reviewer and writer alike are unfathomable and illogical.

CHAPTER 1

What Goes Around Comes Around
Revenge is Best Served Cole

Ethan Cole was the kind of man who made people uneasy, though they couldn't always put their finger on why. He moved through the world with the grace of someone who knew he was more intelligent than most and wasn't above using it. His sharp suits and perfectly tailored coats screamed success, but something cold lurked behind the polished surface, like a snake coiled just out of sight.

He was famous, of course—his best-selling crime novels had made him a household name. Critics praised his ability to create villains so chilling they felt real, their motivations complex, their crimes disturbingly detailed. Too detailed, some whispered now. The way his pen captured the minutiae of murder, the visceral imagery that danced on the page —it was almost as if he'd lived it.

Cole's face was one people recognized from book covers and literary interviews: lean and angular, with a jawline sharp enough to cut glass and eyes the color of a winter storm. But those eyes were empty, detached, as though he was always studying the person before him, cataloging their weaknesses for later use. His charm was undeniable, his voice smooth as whiskey, but it was the kind of charm that made you check your wallet—or lock your door— after he left the room.

The suspicions had started quietly, a murmur in the wake of his estranged wife's disappearance. Then came the discovery of another body—a journalist who'd been writing a profile on him, found murdered in a manner hauntingly similar to the climax of his latest novel. Now, Ethan Cole was at the center of a media frenzy, his name splashed across headlines in a way that had nothing to do with book sales.

To the public, he played the role of the wronged genius, calm under scrutiny, always ready with a soundbite about artistic integrity. But behind closed doors, those who knew him best had seen the cracks: the flash of temper, the way his smile never quite reached his eyes. Ethan Cole wasn't just a writer who could imagine the darkest corners of the human psyche—he might be living proof of them.

Ten years earlier in Grad School at the U of M Ethan Cole's hatred of reviews and reviewers started rooted in a complex interplay of personal experience and professional frustration. At the heart of his hatred is a sense of betrayal stemming from his early encounters with literary criticism. When he first entered the world of publishing, filled with hope and excitement, he was eager to share his stories and his voice. Yet, the reviews that trickled in felt like cold water poured over his dreams, each critique puncturing the fragile balloon of his confidence.

For Cole and other Authors, reviewers are not merely critics; they're gatekeepers wielding an almost tyrannical power over Authors' lives and careers. With the stroke of a pen, they could elevate or demolish the very essence of a writer's work. The arbitrary nature of their judgments infuriated him. He believed that many reviewers lacked the depth of understanding or the empathy needed to appreciate the nuances of a well-crafted story. Instead of celebrating the art of storytelling, they often reduced it to a checklist of flaws, prioritizing technicalities over emotional resonance. To him, this felt like a betrayal of the very spirit of literature.

He grew increasingly frustrated with the reviewers' tendency to prioritize sensationalism over substance, relishing the spectacle of tearing a work apart rather than engaging thoughtfully with its themes. Reviews became a litany of petty criticisms, focusing on trivial details rather than the heart of the narrative. In their quest for clicks and followers, it was as if reviewers had lost sight of what truly mattered in storytelling: the ability to connect with readers, evoke emotion, and transport them to another world. They reveled in their power, using it to bolster their egos rather than support and improved their craft.

Cole's feelings grew as he noticed a troubling trend: reviewers often celebrated mediocrity while panning true artistic endeavors. He watched as lesser-known authors received accolades for formulaic plots and clichéd characters, while his work, which he poured his heart and soul into, was dismissed with a few harsh sentences. It felt deeply unjust, as though the literary landscape was filled with shallow waters while he was drowning.

Beyond the professional frustrations, there was a personal element to his hatred. Many of his peers, whom he had considered friends, had joined the chorus of reviewers, echoing the same tired criticisms and diminishing his accomplishments. The betrayal stung, turning what could have been

camaraderie into resentment. He felt isolated in his artistic vision, surrounded by a community that seemed more interested in tearing down than building up. For many it was all about money.

In his darkest moments, Ethan came to view reviewers as simple predators, lurking in the shadows, ready to pounce on the vulnerabilities of authors. Each review felt like a personal attack, a reflection of their insecurities rather than an honest assessment of his work. The more he reflected on their motivations, the more he became convinced that they thrived on their power over creators—like vultures feeding on the carcasses of artistic ambition and accomplishment. To him they were vermin.

This simmering hatred drove him to extreme thoughts, a yearning for revenge against those who had belittled his journey. Each negative review felt like a weight dragging him down, an anchor in a sea of mediocrity. In the quiet hours of the night, he would replay their words, the sting of their

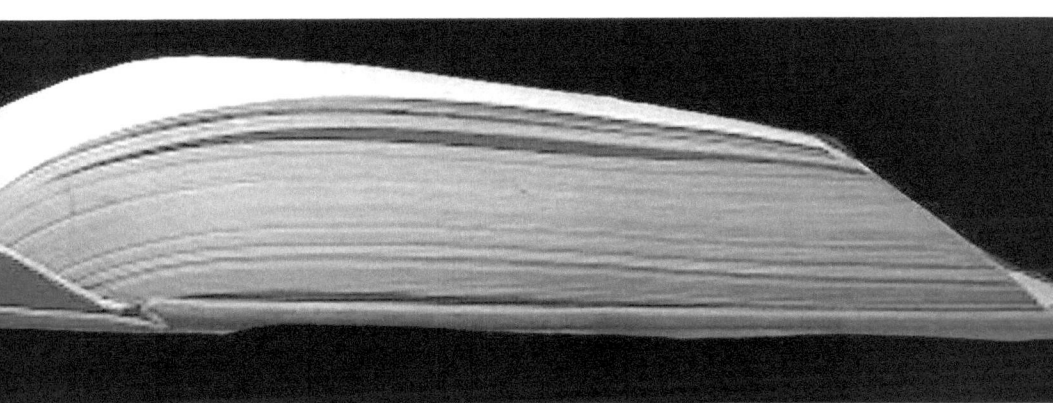

dismissals igniting a fire within him. He envisioned a world where he could silence their voices, where his stories could stand unblemished by their cruel scrutiny and cheap shots.

Ethan's hatred of reviews and reviewers was not just a reaction to criticism; it was a battle cry, a deep-seated rebellion against a system that he believed valued judgment over understanding, noise over substance. It fueled his every word and action, shaping the narrative of his life as he plotted a way to reclaim his voice and, in doing so, challenge the very nature of literary critique itself.

His disdain for reviewers ran deep, a sentiment that had plagued and only intensified with time. To him, they were nothing more than talentless leeches, a cadre of critics who hid behind the safety of their keyboards, wielding their opinions like weapons against those brave enough to bare their souls through the written word.

He believed these reviewers had never known the struggles of crafting a novel from scratch, sweating day and night over a small passage in a novel, the  painstaking hours spent molding characters and plots, pouring heart and soul into each sentence. They didn't understand the vulnerability involved in sharing one's work with the world, nor did they appreciate the artistry in the delicate balance of prose. In his eyes, they were armchair critics, incapable of producing anything of value themselves. They merely skimmed the surface of a book, mainly offering negative judgments that were as superficial as their understanding of the writing and story telling craft.

Cole felt a simmering rage whenever he encountered their reviews. Their scathing remarks struck him as cruel and unearned, fueled by envy rather than genuine critique. To him, it was clear: if they had any real talent or creativity, they would be creating instead of critiquing. They reveled in tearing down the efforts of others while lacking the courage to put pen to paper themselves, hiding behind anonymity and anonymity's false sense of authority.

Most people call the literary world almost as sleazy as the Music business. The manipulation of the book review process by publishers, how the majority of reviewers have never written a word unless it's criticizing an author, and the reliance of Amazon on a review system that is clearly broken and puts self-published independent authors at a disadvantage and allows for revenge reviews from competitors and ex-wives alike. He remembered a meeting he had with a woman 'in the know' about the publishing game years before.

The door to the dimly lit café swung open with a dull creak, letting in a gust of fall air, and struggling independent author Ethan Cole clutched his laptop bag tightly as he stepped inside, shaking off the cold. He scanned the room for his meeting— someone had promised him insight into the shadowy world of publishing reviews, and he wasn't going to waste the chance. Nobody needed to tell Cole about reviews and how they could be the Achilles Heal of any author.

In the corner, a woman waved at him. She was older, perhaps in her mid-forties, with short, silver-streaked hair and a face lined not with age but with disdain. Her name was Elise Rader, once a top-tier literary agent at a major East Coast publishing house and former Kindle Direct Publishing (KDP) Manager, now an outcast after her scathing tell-all article in the New York Times. It was a tell-all about the publishing industry and it burned every bridge she'd ever built. But now she enjoyed being the malcontent outcast.

"Ethan Cole?" she asked as he approached.

"That's me," he replied, sliding into the booth opposite her. "How are you doing?"

Elise took a sip of her black coffee and gestured for him to do the same with the cup waiting for him. "You said you wanted to know about reviews. How deep do you want to go?"

Cole hesitated. He wasn't sure what he had expected —some vague advice on how to improve his own ratings, maybe—but Elise's tone suggested something far darker. It was rare to have someone so experienced come clean about the dirt in publishing.

"Deep enough to understand why my books, which I spent years writing, get obliterated by a review before it even has a chance to find an audience," he said. "And why the same thing seems to happen to every indie author I know. It's almost a conspiracy!"

Elise leaned back in her chair and folded her arms. "Ah. So you're looking for the real truth about the 'review economy.' This is 110% confidential and I will deny having had this conversation, kay? Let me start with this: the system was never designed for you. The 'big A' does not care about Authors."

"What do you mean?" he asked.

"Amazon / KDP," she said, her voice dripping with venom, "the so-called 'world's largest bookstore' doesn't care about writers. It and its advanced computer algorithm care about one thing oand one thing only... sales. And reviews—whether they're genuine, fake, or revenge-driven—are just another lever to push products. For self-published authors like you, it's simply a rigged game. You're playing poker against a dealer who's already stacked the deck against you and every indie Author."

Cole frowned. "I thought reviews were supposed to be about the readers. Honest feedback from people who actually read the book. They are to help, right?"

Elise laughed, a bitter sound. "Honest feedback? Help? That's adorable. I love it when you try to do comedy! Let me break it down for you. Traditional publishers have entire departments dedicated 24/7 to ensuring their books get glowing reviews. They cultivate relationships with influential reviewers, pay for premium visibility, and, if necessary, manufacture praise."

"Manufactured praise?" he probed.

"Fake reviews, sweetheart. They're everywhere. Even the 'legit' ones are often written by freelancers who've been paid under the table with cash, trips, and merchandise. And the reviewers who work for literary magazines? Forget about it! Most of them haven't written an unkind or positive word in years —unless it's to destroy some author who dared criticize them or 'the system.'"

Cole shook his head. "But what about the readers? Real readers?"

"They're the wildcard," Elise admitted. "But even they're not as free as you think. Algorithms decide which books get visibility, and those computers are fed by reviews. If a book doesn't hit a certain threshold of stars within its first week, it's basically dead in the water. Sadly, no amount of organic readership can really save it after that, no matter how good the book is. Sad really."

Cole felt a chill that had nothing to do with the weather. "So what am I supposed to do? Fake my own reviews?"

Elise leaned forward, her expression serious. "You wouldn't be the first. I know authors who've created dozens of fake Amazon accounts to leave glowing reviews on their own books. But that's risky. If Amazon catches you, they'll blacklist you and your books. No warnings, no appeals, and no royalties!"

"And if I don't play the game?" he asked.

"Then you're at the mercy of the system," Elise said. "And that system allows *anyone* with a grudge to torpedo your book or career. Competitors, bitter ex-spouses, random trolls who get off on being negative —they all have the same power as a genuine reader who actually read the book and loved your work."

Cole stared into his coffee, the bitter scent suddenly overwhelming. He thought about the review that had tanked his debut novel, 'Death on the Page'. The reviewer, a local newspaper reviewer named Calvin Reese, had called it "a poorly written, amateurish waste of time." among other things. But the phrasing

had seemed oddly specific, almost personal. He'd always suspected it had come from someone jealous of his modest success. Later he found Reese guilty of plagiarism.

"And self-published authors are the easiest targets," Elise continued, pulling him out of his thoughts. "You don't have a publisher to back you up, no PR team to manage your reputation. You are out there all on your own."

"So what's the solution?" Cole asked, desperate now to make some sense to all of it.

"There isn't one," Elise said bluntly. "Not unless the entire system changes. And that's not going to happen as long as Amazon controls the market. They don't care if the reviews are fair; they care if they drive sales. Traditional publishers can afford to game the system, but indies? You're just collateral damage. The system is engineered not to change."

Cole slumped in his chair. "So what you're saying is... it's basically hopeless."

Elise softened just a little. "Not hopeless. But hard. You have to be relentless. Build your audience one reader at a time. Engage with them directly, outside of platforms like Amazon. And most importantly, don't let the reviews—good or bad—define you. Write because you love it and because the stories demand it, not because you're chasing stars or money," she said.

Cole nodded slowly. It wasn't the answer he'd wanted, but it was the truth. And in a world built on lies, that was something. He knew now why more than more independent authors were ditching the Amazon game and selling direct via their own web sites. As he got up to leave, Elise called after him. "One more thing." He turned back towards her.

"If you ever make it big enough for them to notice you," she said, "don't forget who you are. The moment you start playing their game, you'll lose."

Cole thanked her and walked out into the cold night both literally and figuratively, her words ringing in his ears. He didn't know if he had it in him to fight the system. But one thing was certain: he wasn't going to let it break him and there was one reviewer in particular that needed to be dealt with. And he would.

The wind whipped around him as he made his way home, laptop bag slung over his shoulder. Somewhere out there, he knew, was a reader who would love his books. All he had to do was find them. And maybe, just maybe, that would be enough. But the unfair review from one man years before stuck in his craw and his hatred continued to grow. Somebody needed to put Reese in his place and extract a certain price for basically destroying a career.

Even now every time he read a negative review, it felt like a personal attack—a reminder that his passion was being dismissed by those who didn't have the guts to pursue their dreams. The irony gnawed at him: these reviewers, often claiming to promote literary quality, instead thrived on the destruction of artists' dreams. They inflated their own egos at the expense of writers who bled onto the pages while their own talents languished in obscurity. And the bottom line of course is money.

In Cole's mind, book reviewers were nothing but parasites, feasting on the success and failures of others without ever contributing to the literary landscape themselves. Their barbs, often laced with condescension, echoed the insecurities he had battled throughout his career. He couldn't help but view their words as a reflection of their own failures, a misguided attempt to elevate themselves by dragging others down. They wielded their pens like swords, slashing at the fabric of creativity and innovation. They offer nothing of value to authors.

This resentment simmered beneath the surface, morphing into a consuming rage that ultimately drove him to the edge. It wasn't just about the reviews; it was about the principle of artistic integrity being undermined by those too cowardly to create themselves. He vowed that if ever given the opportunity, he would confront these self-proclaimed critics, challenging them to put their money where their mouth was and produce something of worth themselves. Fat chance.

Deep down, Cole knew that this hatred was as corrosive as it was consuming, yet he found it hard to shake. He clung to the idea that by exposing the hypocrisy of these reviewers and the system itself, he could validate his own worth as a writer. The anger fueled him, pushing him to extremes and clouding his judgment. He saw himself as a warrior battling against a tide of mediocrity, fighting for the honor of those who dared to create in a world where critics and the public thrived on negativity.

12th Annual Kindle Book Awards

2023

Kindle Book Awards

Honorable Mention

12th Annual Kindle Book Awards

READERS' FAVORITE®

BOOK AWARD WINNER

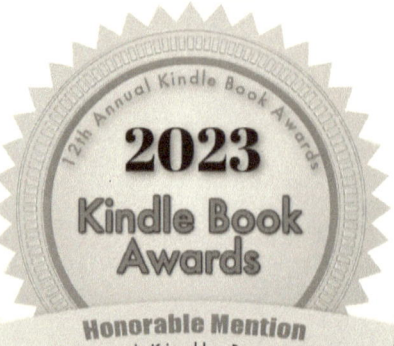

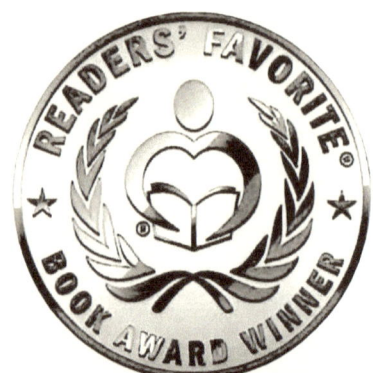

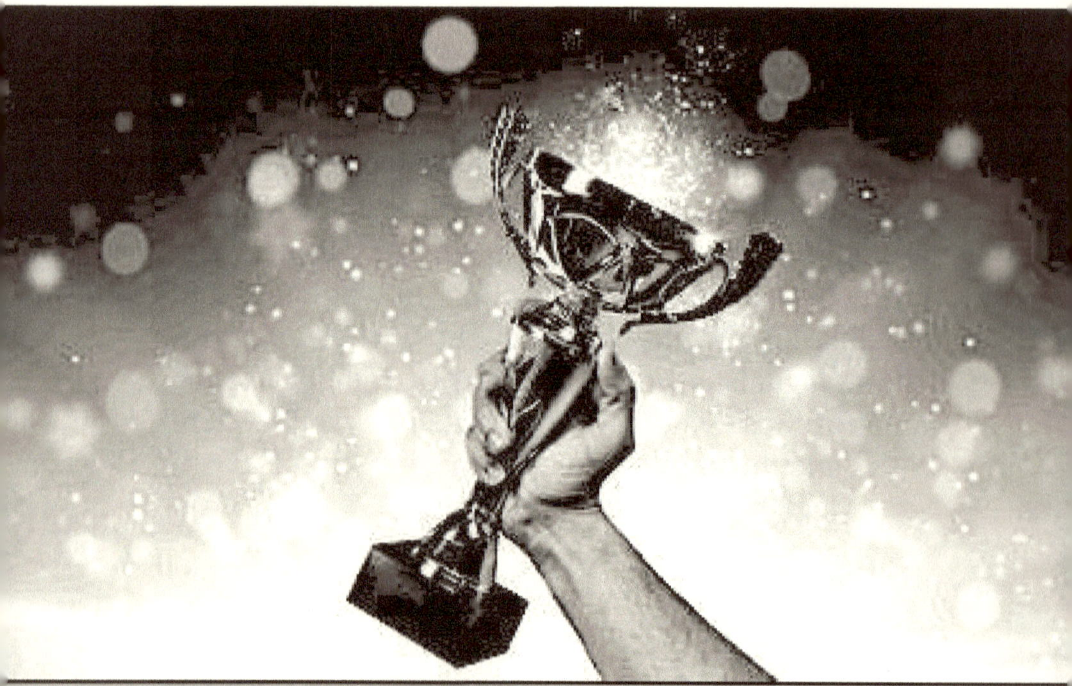

INTERNATIONAL IMPACT BOOK AWARDS

WINNER

THE GOOD MORNING AMERICA BOOK CLUB

A GMA BOOK CLUB PICK!

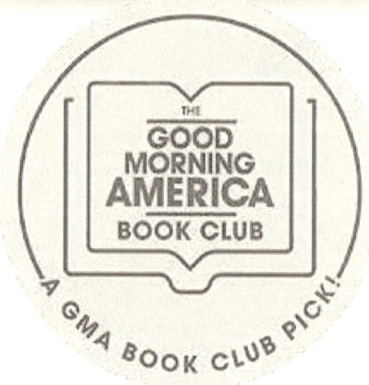

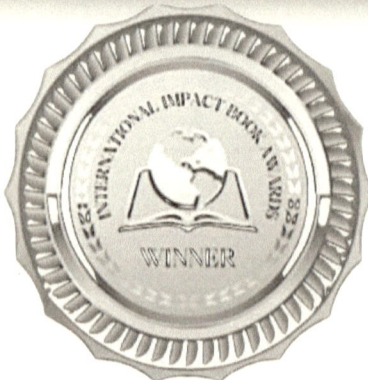

CHAPTER 2

The Hate Society
Awarded Mediocrity

C alvin Reese's opinion of Ethan Cole was always far from flattering. To him, Ethan was a hack writer—a once-promising talent who had squandered his potential by resting on the success of a single hit book. Reese viewed Cole as a relic of a bygone era, clinging to the fleeting fame of his debut novel while failing to evolve or produce anything of substance since.

In Reese's eyes, Cole's initial success had been nothing more than a stroke of luck, a fluke that had drawn the attention of readers and critics alike. He felt that Ethan had not only missed the mark on subsequent projects but had also lost the spark that had initially captivated audiences. It was as if the writer had become complacent, content to bask in the glory of past achievements rather than daring to innovate or challenge himself.

Reese's disdain for Cole deepened as he observed the author's reluctance to embrace change. He believed that writers needed to continuously push their boundaries, experimenting with new ideas, styles, and themes. In contrast, Ethan seemed trapped in a formula that had once worked, recycling tired tropes and familiar characters instead of taking risks that might yield greater artistic rewards.

To Reese, the world of literature was unforgiving, a space where only those willing to grow and adapt could thrive. He felt that Ethan was an embodiment of everything wrong with contemporary writing: a figure who had garnered attention but failed to deliver the substance needed to warrant lasting recognition. He had little respect for what he deemed a "one-hit wonder," feeling that Cole's work was a pale imitation of true literary brilliance.

When Reese published his review, he felt a sense of responsibility to the literary community—to expose what he saw as the mediocrity of Ethan Cole. He believed that readers deserved better than the recycled narratives and predictable plots that Cole had come to represent. His critique was sharp, unyielding, and laced with the conviction that someone needed to hold Cole accountable for his perceived stagnation.

In Reese's view, there was an insidious nature to complacency in writing, a betrayal of the very craft that demanded authenticity and creativity. He believed that every writer had a duty to honor their readers by continually striving for excellence and innovation. In his mind, Ethan had fallen short of this obligation, allowing his initial success to dull his ambition and diminish his voice.

The animosity simmered within Reese, fueled by a combination of professional rivalry and a personal sense of integrity. He saw Cole's success as a threat to the integrity of the literary world, a dangerous precedent that allowed mediocrity to flourish in a space that should be reserved for brilliance. His words in the review reflected this belief, crafted with a sharpness designed to cut through the complacency he despised.

Ultimately, Reese's feelings toward Cole were rooted in a deep-seated belief that true artistry required relentless dedication and a willingness to confront one's limitations. He viewed Ethan as a cautionary tale, a reminder of the dangers of complacency in a profession that thrived on evolution and growth. In his mind, Ethan had chosen the easy path, and for that, he deserved not just criticism but a reckoning.

Calvin Reese's view of Ethan Cole was steeped in contempt, a reaction not merely born of professional rivalry but fueled by a profound belief in the sanctity of the literary craft. To Reese, Cole represented everything wrong with the contemporary writing landscape—an author who had stumbled upon a modicum of success and then proceeded to bask in its glow, effectively coasting on the laurels of his past achievement. In Reese's eyes, Ethan was a hack writer, a label he wore like a badge of honor whenever he mentioned Cole in conversations.

The crux of Reese's disdain lay in his belief that Ethan's debut novel, a surprising bestseller that had captured the hearts of many, was nothing more than a lucky break. From Reese's perspective, Cole had struck gold in a moment when the literary gods favored him, and rather than seizing that opportunity to grow and diversify his work, he had instead retreated into a comfortable bubble of mediocrity. The initial success, to Reese, was indicative of a man who had been at the right place at the right time with the right story, rather than a true talent who'd earned their place through relentless dedication and a commitment to the craft.

Best Fiction
Book
'Death on the Page'
by
Ethan Cole

Ethan's subsequent works, which had garnered mixed reviews, only served to solidify Reese's convictions. The writer seemed to cling stubbornly to familiar themes, rehashing old characters and predictable plots that offered little in the way of innovation. Each new release felt like a shadow of the first as if Ethan were unwilling or unable to break free from the constraints of his earlier success. For Reese, this stagnation was not just disappointing; it was an affront to the very notion of artistic integrity.

Reese had little patience for what he perceived as Ethan's lack of ambition. He believed that a true writer should constantly challenge themselves, pushing the boundaries of their creativity and exploring uncharted territories within their own artistry. In Reese's view, literature was a dynamic field that required ongoing evolution; stagnation was not merely a setback—it was a betrayal of readers who craved fresh perspectives and innovative storytelling. He often mused about how writers who failed to adapt inevitably faded into obscurity, becoming nothing more than a footnote in literary history. The publishing world's 'One Hit Wonders'.

When Reese published his scathing review of Cole's latest offering, it was more than just an opinion; it was an indictment of complacency itself. Reese felt a moral imperative to speak out, to shine a light on what he deemed the mediocrity of a once-promising author. He believed that by challenging Cole, he was not just elevating his own voice but also defending the artistic integrity of the literary community. His critique was sharp, unyielding, and infused with a passionate belief that readers deserved more than a rehashed version of a tired narrative.

Every word he penned in that review was laced with conviction. He took aim at what he perceived as Cole's laziness, highlighting the missed opportunities for character development and the reliance on clichés. To Reese, each lackluster plot twist was a betrayal of the trust that readers placed in authors to provide them with compelling stories that challenged their intellect and emotions. His words sought to unravel the facade that Cole had built around himself—a facade that Reese saw as a thin veil draped over the reality of an artist who had lost his way or was never that much to start with.

Reese often thought about the nature of talent and what it meant to be a writer. In his mind, true artistry was not just about creating a successful book; it was about a lifelong commitment to growth, exploration, and, most importantly, risk-taking. Ethan, in Reese's eyes, had turned his back on these ideals. He had chosen the easy route, opting for familiarity over innovation, comfort over challenge.

As Reese reflected on his own journey as a writer, he felt a mixture of envy and pity towards Ethan. He envied the success that had come so easily to Cole, yet he also pitied him for the path he had taken. In a world where so many struggled to be heard, Ethan had been given a platform and had squandered it. The reality was harsh, and Calvin couldn't shake the feeling that by allowing mediocrity to flourish, the literary world was ultimately diminished.

Reese's sharp critiques weren't just personal; they were rooted in a desire for accountability in a profession that he held sacred. He wanted to hold Ethan accountable not just for his own work but for the impact his complacency had on aspiring writers everywhere. In Reese's mind, it was a moral duty to challenge those who had the talent but chose to remain stagnant, allowing the art form to suffer.

Ethan Cole, as far as Reese was concerned, was a cautionary tale. He represented a dangerous precedent in a profession that thrived on evolution and growth. In every negative review he penned, Reese aimed not only to dismantle Cole's reputation but to ignite a conversation about the need for writers to embrace change, to push themselves beyond their limits, and to honor the craft with a fierce commitment to excellence. The status quo was simply not good enough. To Reese, the literary world needed warriors willing to fight against complacency, and he was more than ready to take up that cause. But for him everything was transactional.

Recently Cole was doing a book signing at a major book event, with Reese also there signing his new 'Death Pages' novel. They were placed within view of each other right across the aisle. Having looked over Reese's new title Cole was livid about the fact that Reese basically stole his story from Grad School and was now publishing it as his own.

Cole starred at him, noting Reese hadn't aged well in the intervening years since college. Perhaps the evil comments he made about other people's writing were showing up on his face. The idea now percolating in Cole's head was that it would be a real shame if Reese who lived by the written word, he should also die by the written word. One of two things would be true by the time the sun went down; one is that Cole would make Reese pay and the other was that he would somehow try to change the system. The idea was formed then and there.

10th Precinct Squad Room

CHAPTER 3

Critical Hangover
It's Nothing Personal

The morning sunlight glared through Calvin Reese's apartment window, pooling over stacks of manuscripts, unopened mail, and half-read novels. His desk was cluttered with the detritus of a life spent judging others' work, the pages bleeding red ink from his annotations and jottings, each one sharper than the last. He stirred his coffee with the same mechanical indifference with which he approached his reviews, tapping the spoon on the side of the mug before setting it down; his thoughts were elsewhere and far away.

Calvin Reese built his career on tearing others down. His name was synonymous with razor-sharp critiques and the kind of literary dissections that left even the most celebrated authors bleeding. He was the critic authors dreaded, the one who could turn a best seller into a punchline with a single scathing review. And Calvin loved his growing reputation.

He was a tall, wiry man with a perpetually smug expression, as though he was always privy to a joke no one else could understand. His gray eyes gleamed behind thin, wire-rimmed glasses, sharp and judgmental, missing nothing. His suits were always expensive, impeccably tailored, and just understated enough to suggest he cared about appearances but wouldn't stoop to admit it.

Reese had started as a failed novelist himself, which, according to the literary circles, only made his criticism more venomous. He had a talent for finding an author's softest spot—the rookie mistake, the sentimental line, the overused trope—and twisting the knife until the wound festered. Authors whispered about him in greenrooms and at book launches, equal parts loathing him and fearing his next essay.

It wasn't just his reviews that made people hate him —it was his swagger. Reese didn't just critique; he annihilated. And he enjoyed every second of it. His lectures were standing-room only, where he eviscerated the literary canon and contemporary darlings with equal fervor. His own book on criticism, The Art of Destruction, was a bestseller and required reading in MFA programs, though many students read it through gritted teeth.

So when Calvin Reese was found dead before his time—no one was truly surprised. The list of suspects was longer than most novels. There were the famous authors he'd humiliated in print, the debut writers he'd crushed before they'd even started, and the publishers whose livelihoods he'd jeopardized with his acidic prose. The irony, of course, was that Calvin Reese had always claimed that literature should reflect the darkness of

humanity. In the end, his life had become the perfect murder mystery—one he'd never get to review.

Reese had barely glanced at a copy of his book Cole had thrust into his hands at the signing event the night before. 'It's a peace offering," said Cole as he presented it to him. He purchased the single leather bound collector's copy of Reeses' theft at an obscure bookshop across town instead of online where it would be too easy for police to trace purchases. The carved hard leather cover had tons of nooks and crannies where a poison could hide. And Cole was familiar with Reese's habit of fondling these "collector's editions" where he would usually repeatedly run his hands across the cover and pages.

Cole's appearance had troubled him. The man he knew from college was intense, standing in the reader's line with an almost forced politeness that had struck him as both odd and a little desperate. That smirk. Reese couldn't quite shake it.

As he sipped his coffee, Reese reached for the leather-bound book, 'Death Pages,' from the night before. Flipping through its pages with a faint curl of satisfaction, he started to remember another book from back in grad school. He'd savaged it in a review in the local arts magazine and newspaper, a response he'd written after slogging through its tedious plot twists and overwrought metaphors. But in Reese's mind his book was totally different than the one Cole had written back then.

"Another bestseller for the mindless masses," he'd called it, a comment that had earned him both admiration and a flurry of furious messages from Cole's most dedicated fans and his lawyers. Reese almost chuckled at the memory; a faint twist of satisfaction came to him. He had remembered the book but not the Author... but what he did recall was that the book's author was an unoriginal hack.

But now, as he leafed through the book, he noticed something odd. A peculiar scent, faint but lingering, as though the pages had been dusted with something metallic. He dismissed it, chalking it up to the printer or the ink or perhaps his Bourbon intake from the night before. He'd been in this business

long enough to know that sometimes, books, like the Author's, simply came with strange odors.

About an hour later the faint prickling in his fingertips barely registered at first—a dull, tingling sensation that felt more like nerves than anything concrete. His hands had been bothering him lately, he reasoned. The doctor had mentioned stress and advised him to rest, but Reese dismissed it as he did all unsolicited advice. Stress was for other people. He knew exactly who he was and what he did best.

With a sigh, he set the book aside and grabbed another manuscript from the pile of titles up for review. The book's first chapter dragged on, an uninspired attempt at suspense that only managed to bore him. He felt a wave of irritation rising and massaging his temples, feeling the start of a headache nudging at the edges of his mind. He reached for his coffee but set it down, uncharacteristically nauseous. Strange. Calvin Reese didn't get sick; he never did. But as he sat back, an odd weariness settled over him, a deep-seated exhaustion that seeped into his bones.

He looked at his hands, flexing his fingers. The tingling had grown sharper now, a pins-and-needles sensation that crawled up his wrists. Maybe he needed to take a break and get some fresh air. The apartment felt stifling, the clutter pressing in on him more than usual. Calvin pushed back from his desk, shrugging on his coat with a wince as his joints protested the movement. He slipped 'Death Pages' into his bag, intending to return to it later. As much as he loved the book, there was something about the smug smile of the reader who gave it to him at the signing the night before, it was… unsettling.

Reese made his way down the street, pulling his collar up against the brisk wind. The city was alive with its usual frenzy, but today it felt louder and harsher, the sounds jarring his already frayed nerves. Every step felt heavier than the last, his legs unsteady. He stopped to rest against a lamppost, breathing deeply, though each breath felt thin, as though he were gasping through a narrow straw. The cafe was only 2 more blocks and he frequented it religiously twice a week on Mondays and Fridays.

"Are you alright, sir?" A woman's voice broke through his stupor, and he turned to see a young woman watching him with concern. Her eyes flickered over his pale face, the sheen of sweat gathering on his forehead. Reese nodded, brushing her off with a muttered assurance that he was fine, though he knew he looked anything but.

When he made it to his usual Cafe, he collapsed into a booth by the window, looking out at the street with a detachment that bordered on the surreal. The world moved around him, bustling and oblivious, while his own thoughts blurred, weighed down by a fog he couldn't shake. The weird tingling from last night and this morning had crept up his arms now, lingering in his joints… it was like when a limb falls asleep. Meanwhile, his head throbbed like a samba trio in time with his pulse. His vision blurred for a split second, a wave of nausea washing over him so sudden and strong that he had to grip the edge of the table to steady himself. And then there was the fever that was growing. His mind went blank for a second.

"Mr. Reese?" A voice from the counter called his name, and he forced a smile, standing shakily to retrieve his order. He could feel the barista's eyes on him as he took his coffee, his hand shaking slightly as he grasped the cup. He

45

hated the vulnerability of it, hated that he looked frail or intoxicated. But he pushed down the unease, swallowing a mouthful of scalding coffee as if it could burn away whatever strange sickness had taken hold of him.

Back at his table, he absently opened the special edition book Cole had given him the day before… It was one of the rare limited editions—a pristine volume with a gilded spine, the kind that Reese, for all his vitriol, couldn't refuse. Sitting in his booth his fingers lingering on the pages as he flipped through them. The tingling grew sharper, a negative feeling that now seemed to radiate from the book itself. He shut it with a grimace, rubbing his hands against his thighs as if to dispel the feeling.

As he sat there, an unnerving thought slipped into his mind, whispering with a quiet insistence. 'What if... I have cancer!?' he thought. But as he was otherwise in great shape Reese dismissed it, shaking his head at his own paranoia. It was just the flu.

He chuckled softly to himself, though the sound came out strained and hollow. And yet, as he sat there, staring down at his shaking hands, a single thought persisted, lingering like the taste of hot sauce on his tongue... why would Cole come to him with a 'peace offering' after all these years? Reese could not really recall their past in school. The years of high-society cocktail parties and boozy press receptions had not been kind to Reese's memory.

CHAPTER 4

Tool of Hate!
Pages of Revenge

T he reoccurring memory played in Ethan Cole's mind like a film he'd watched too many times. The dream was always the same… It was a rainy evening, the kind of night where the city's streets blurred into watercolor smudges beneath the streetlights. Reese ducked into his favorite cafe to escape the drizzle, the scent of damp concrete and burnt coffee mingling in the air. He felt like shit.

And like the night before Calvin Reese was, seated at his usual booth by the window. The critic was hunched over a tablet, his wire-rimmed glasses reflecting the glow of the screen as he typed furiously, no doubt crafting his next literary takedown. Reese didn't see Cole across the cafe at first, too absorbed in his work to notice anyone least of all the man sitting there watching him with a strange mix of disdain and calm.

Cole sat in the dimly lit corner of the café, his fingers drumming rhythmically on the edge of his notebook. The scent of espresso mingled with the smell of damp paper from the day's newspapers, all of it blurring into the background as he watched. The barista called out orders with a bored indifference, and people shuffled in and out, each of them oblivious to his quiet vigil. After some time Cole approached him slowly.

"Calvin, fancy meeting you here again," he said, his voice sarcastic but almost pleasant. Reese looked up, his lips curling into a smirk the moment he saw him.

"Mr. Cole," Reese replied, his tone dripping with condescension. "Still penning those melodramas?" He was the master of the back-handed compliment.

Cole didn't rise to the bait. Instead, he motioned to the book on the table, "So are you enjoying the book I gave ya? A little token of my... gratitude for all your feedback on my work over the years," he said.

Reese chuckled, a dry, brittle sound, as he picked up the book. He flipped it open, inspecting the signature scrawled inside the front cover. *"To Calvin Reese,"* he read, *"What goes around, comes around! Sincerely, Ethan Cole."* It was only now that Cole wondered about the wisdom of signing it. But he was happy that it seemed Reese had finally recognized him from their time in Ann Arbor at Michigan.

"Thanks for the book. But you know that flattery won't save you from my honesty," Reese said, his eyes narrowing slightly.

"That's no fun and I wouldn't expect it to," Cole replied, a faint smile tugging at the corner of his lips. "But perhaps you'll find this next one of mine worth your time. It's all about revenge…"

Reese waved him off with a dismissive gesture, already returning to his work with the gift book remaining on his table.

"You take care of yourself now," Cole said, returning to his booth without looking back.

He felt a faint thrill coursing through him as he walked away, a dark exhilaration of anticipation he couldn't quite name. Cole decided to wait a bit more his fingers tightening around the edge of his table, alone in the present. The recent events had been calculated, deliberate, and to him, utterly necessary. Reese had underestimated his situation and Ethan loved seeing him in discomfort.

The low hum of conversation and the soft hiss of the grill and espresso machine continued blending into a familiar and comforting soundtrack. The rain continued, a steady drizzle that painted the cafe windows in streaks of gray. Cole had chosen the cafe deliberately: a neutral, familiar and unassuming space where no one would question two literary figures crossing paths. Reese was there at least twice a week and often a lot more. He would perch in his favorite corner booth, his laptop glowing in the dim light, a half-empty cappuccino cooling by his side.

Cole flashed back to the night before when he had walked in carrying the book, his hands steady despite the storm outside and the one brewing inside him. The leather-bound copy of Reeses' book felt heavier than it should have, its weight a reminder of its heavy, carved, one of a kind leather cover.

Reese looked up as Cole approached again, his expression a mixture of surprise and disdain. "Cole!" he said, leaning back in his chair. "Again?! To what do I owe this honor?"

"Just spreading the good will," Cole said.

Reese chuckled, a dry, cutting sound. "Goodwill? From you? Interesting…" He picked up the book again, his fingers brushing over the leather cover, and Cole's breath increased for the briefest few seconds.

"Signed, of course," Reese said, flipping it open. He skimmed the inscription and smirked, that smug, insufferable smirk Cole had imagined wiping off his face a thousand times.

"I thought you might appreciate a personalized touch," Cole said, his voice calm and measured. "It's a good one and I hope you do well," he lied.

Reese laughed again, the sound grating, "Well, thanks. I suppose even you can surprise me now and then." He began coughing and didn't stop for a long time.

The Old Village Cafe

Cole stayed at the table only long enough to see Reese run his fingers across the cover and along the edges of the pages, thumbing through the book like the one book he'd written was already beneath his interest. He had already moved on.

For the first time in years, Cole allowed himself to smile. He was a man who had mastered the art of waiting. As time slipped by in the small cafe, he could feel the weight of anticipation settling over him like a heavy fog. The muted hum of conversation surrounded him, punctuated by the occasional hiss of the espresso machine, but all of it faded into the background as he fixated on Reese. His fingers drummed lightly against the table, a rhythm echoing the frantic beating of his heart and the cafe wall-clock ticking off the minutes. Ethan left the cafe before the coffee in Reese's cup cooled completely. Outside, the rain had soaked through his coat, but he didn't feel it. His mind buzzed with the thought of Reese's sneering voice, and his arrogant laugh never haunting him again.

The next day it was almost like the groundhog day movie... a complete redo. Cole felt he simply had to be there to see Reese's progress. He glanced at his watch again. Five minutes past noon. Calvin Reese was late. Cole had carefully orchestrated these encounters, wanting to observe the critic's reaction to the very words he had penned. A part of him relished the thought of watching Reese squirm under the weight of his own judgments. The irony was almost poetic—Calvin, who had built a career out of dissecting others, would soon find himself on the wrong end of that scalpel.

The door swung open, and in walked Reese, looking worse than Cole had anticipated. The critic's face was pale, his usually sharp features softened by a sheen of sweat. Ethan's lips curled into a slight smile. Perfect.

Reese staggered to the counter, gripping the edge for support. He mumbled his order of a cappuccino in a hoarse voice, and Cole watched, fascinated as he fumbled with his wallet and then with the sugar and the cup, his hands shaking. The cafe's patrons shifted their attention toward Reese, concern etching on their faces. And Cole felt a surge of satisfaction at his discomfort. To him Reese looked, for the first time, vulnerable—like an aging actor forced to confront his own mortality under unforgiving lights. Cole wondered if the critic had even realized what was happening to him. Would he understand that every sting in his limbs and wave of nausea should have been anticipated?

He was here because he wanted to see Reese's face at that moment, to witness the horror of realization. But that would be too risky. He knew that. This had to look like a natural, tragic collapse. A sudden stroke, perhaps, or a heart attack—a poetic irony for a man who'd preyed so ruthlessly on the many vulnerabilities of authors.

Cole sipped his espresso, the bitter liquid grounding him, sharpening his focus. He could see Calvin's body language shift, the tension radiating from him as he struggled to steady his breathing. This was a man used to wielding words like weapons, and now was powerless, trapped in a story he can't control.

"Calvin?" Ethan called out, his voice smooth and casual, like a knife gliding through butter. Reese's head snapped up, his eyes narrowing as they tried to focus and meet Ethan's gaze. This time there was no recognition there, only confusion and fear.

"Do you remember me from Grad School and the book signing on Monday night? I'm Ethan Cole," he said introducing himself again and leaning forward slightly. "I see you've been enjoying the special copy of the book I gave you. It's a penetrating novel that's for sure," he said.

Reese's expression of confusion twisted into a grimace, his lips forming a thin line. "I didn't think authors were allowed to stalk reviewers," he said his voice hoarse and without its usual arrogant tone.

"Are you feeling alright?" Cole chuckled softly, taking a moment to enjoy his pain and the unfolding drama. "I prefer to think of this all as quality control. You see old friend, reviews have consequences. They shape perceptions, mold careers. I simply wanted us both to witness the impact of your words first hand. What goes around... comes around," Cole said. "Wow, you really don't look well at all!"

Reese opened his mouth to respond, but the words caught in his throat. His face flushed with fever now around 102, and his hands gripped the table as if it were the only thing keeping him upright. As paralysis set in Cole could see the panic creeping into his eyes, the realization that something was unalterably and drastically wrong.

Twenty minutes passed, and Reese seemed to be struggling more with each breath. He hunched over his cup, his head sinking into his hands, his fingers massaging his temples. Cole wondered if the critic was starting to think the sickness wasn't just a fluke. Was it?

"Sir, Are you alright?" Cole asked again from two tables over, feigning concern, though the smirk tugging at his lips probably betrayed him.

Reese gasped, his breaths now coming in short, desperate bursts. He leaned forward, hands clenched with his knuckles whitening. "Something's— wrong," he said. Reese's voice was barely a whisper, each ragged breath punctuated by a painful cough.

He struggled to rise from his chair, but his legs buckled beneath him, sending him crashing to the floor of the cafe and hitting his head on the tile floor! The barista rushed over, her voice a panicked blur as she called for someone to dial 911 emergency. Someone else shouted for help and to call 911, but Cole, frozen, just watching the calamity from a front row seat.

Reese's eyes were now wide and frantic, his hand clawing at his throat as though trying to pull something out of his body. It was obvious to Cole and the onlookers that he was deathly ill. It appeared that Reese's arrogance was about to end. Others in the cafe began to worry about if whatever Reese had was catching and some sort of bio hazard.

Cole remained seated, his pulse quickening as the cafe's chaos erupted around them. Patrons jumped to their feet, eyes wide with alarm. As Reese writhed on the ground, his body convulsing, Cole felt an exhilaration wash over him. The man who had wielded the power of critique like a sword was now at the mercy of something he'd never seen coming. The finality of it all was intoxicating, a high that coursed through Cole's veins as he reveled in the poetic justice unfolding before him. It was both satisfying and revolting.

Reese was likely feeling the worst of it by now: a gnawing nausea, tingling limbs, fever and the faintest hint of impending paralysis. His face was now twisted in agony, and for a moment, their eyes met again. This time, there was no confusion, no bravado—only a raw, desperate understanding of the inevitability that surrounded him. Reese seemed to suddenly have a realization that he could die. Cole then leaned closer, lowering his voice to a conspiratorial and confrontational whisper.

"You see, Calvin, this is what happens when you fuck others over and play with fire. You can't destroy peoples lives without repercussions Reese. Karma's real and she's a bitch!" he said.

Cole felt he deserved every miserable symptom he would have on the road to the morgue. Was Reese realizing, in those final moments, that his agony was someone's handiwork? That his obsession with dissecting other people's work had now led someone to dissect him in return?

Then Reese threw up all over his expensive cashmere sweater, the fight rapidly draining from him as his eyes glazed over. It was a beautiful moment for Cole. For Reese, as the life left his body, there was the inkling that his own words had led to his tragic end.

The ambulance arrived minutes later, but by then, Calvin Reese was beyond saving. Paramedics worked frantically, but Cole knew it was all for show. He was gone. As the paramedics worked to save him, the cacophony of shouts and the blare of sirens and 2-way radios filled the cafe. The CPR counts drowning out the whispers of the patrons who were already speculating about the nature of the critic's sudden death. When the ambulance guy

pulled the sheet over Reese's head everyone in the cafe knew he was dead.

In the disorder Cole slipped out of his seat, moving with the calmness of a man who had just finished a thrilling chapter or passage in a novel, leaving behind the chaos of Calvin's demise. He stepped into the brisk fall air outside, feeling the cool wind on his face. The world continued to spin, blissfully unaware of Reese's passing.

Ethan felt a dark satisfaction bloom in his heart. This was the man who had sneered at his work, belittled his years of effort at every turn, and reduced his words to nothing more than fodder for his cruel reviews. Watching him now, struggling and dying on the floor, felt like poetic justice.

As Cole walked away from the cafe, a sense of liberation washed over him. The critic was finally gone, silenced at last, and for the first time in ten years, he felt a spark of hope igniting within him. Perhaps, now, he could write freely, unburdened by the looming shadow of Reeses' criticism. Maybe now the world would see him clearly for what he truly was—a master of his craft, free to create without fear of the haters lurking in the shadows.

In the distance, sirens wailed, but Ethan didn't turn back. He had a story to tell—one that would put his words on the page without the taint of judgment from those who had only ever sought to tear him down. It was time to reclaim his narrative and besides… it was really a hell of a story!

62

CHAPTER 5

The Muse Returns
Death Comes Quick

Ethan Cole barely noticed the bustling streets of downtown as he walked, his mind racing with the adrenaline of his newfound freedom. The chaos he had left behind in the café was quickly fading from his consciousness, replaced by an exhilarating sense of power. The air was crisp and sharp against his skin, invigorating him as he navigated through the throngs of unsuspecting pedestrians.

He rounded the corner onto a quieter street, the noise of the city muffling into a distant hum. A wave of giddiness washed over him as he replayed the events of the last few days in his mind. Calvin Reese was gone, and with him, the crushing weight of the critic's disdain. Ethan felt a real sense of liberation, a release from the shackles that had held him back for far too long.

Yet, amid the exhilaration, a flicker of doubt crept in, whispering that this victory came at a terrible cost. He shook his head, dispelling the thought. "It was necessary", he told himself. Calvin Reese had made a career of dismantling dreams, and in Ethan's

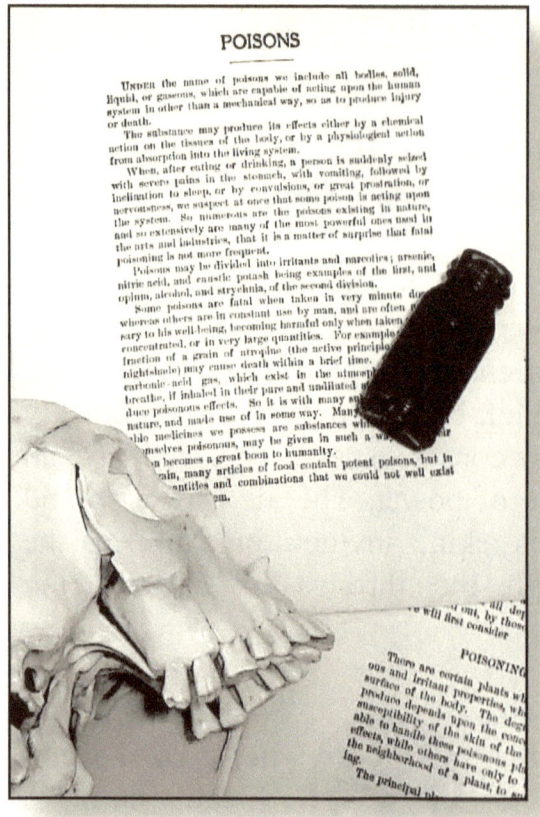

mind, "the world is better off without him!"

He wandered into a nearby park, where the leaves were turning shades of gold and crimson, the beauty of autumn stark against the backdrop of his dark thoughts. In the evening quiet of the park Ethan found a bench and sank into its comforting embrace. He pulled out his notebook, the pages filled with half-formed story ideas, frantic scribbles, and unfiltered thoughts and ideas.

The words flowed effortlessly as he began to write, the thrill of creation surging through him. He crafted scenes where characters faced their demons, where the weight of a single decision could lead to both salvation and destruction. The writing poured out of him, each stroke of the pen feeling like an act of defiance against all the negativity that had once stifled his voice.

But the exhilaration was interrupted by the unwelcome sound of sirens in the distance, a reminder that the chaos of the café had not dissipated entirely. Panic clawed at the edges of his mind, and he forced himself to focus on the page, determined to drown out the noise. Calvin's death was bound to eventually raise questions, and Ethan knew he needed to cover his tracks.

A thought struck him, sharp and clear. He would need to establish an alibi—an unshakeable story that would place him far away from the scene of the crime when the paramedics arrived. He could already envision the headlines: "Prominent Reviewer Found Dead at Local Café—Mystery Surrounds Sudden Collapse!"

Cole's fingers flew across the page, outlining a new narrative where he was the unwitting observer rather than the orchestrator. A last-minute decision to leave the city for a weekend retreat, an innocent excursion to clear his mind, all perfectly timed to coincide with Reese's fatal encounter.

As he wrote, he felt a new character taking shape within him—a man who embraced life's unpredictability, a writer who refused to be held captive by fear. This character would navigate through the chaos of life, overcoming the trials that fate would throw his way. Perhaps he would even face a ruthless critic, giving him the chance to play out his revenge in fiction rather than reality.

His heart raced as he became lost in the story, imagining the twists and turns of a plot that paralleled real life. Yet, in the back of his mind, the sirens continued to wail, a reminder that he was not yet free from the consequences of recent events.
Before he knew it a few hours had passed.

Suddenly, a figure approached from the path, pulling Ethan from his thoughts. It was a woman, her dark hair cascading over her shoulders, her sharp green eyes scanning the park as if searching for something. He felt a jolt of recognition; it was Claire, a former classmate from his writing workshops. They had once shared laughter and discussions about the intricacies of storytelling, but after several harsh reviews from Reese, their paths had diverged.

"Ethan?" she called, her voice cutting through the haze of his thoughts. "Is that you?"

He forced a smile, masking the turmoil beneath the surface. "Claire! Wow what a surprise."
She approached, her brows furrowing in concern as she took a seat beside him. "You look… different. Are you alright?"

"Just busy with my latest project," he replied, gesturing toward his notebook, the pages open to his chaotic scrawl. "You know how it is. The creative process is a bitch and can be a bit all-consuming."

Claire nodded, but the concern remained etched on her face. "I just heard about Calvin Reese. It's shocking, isn't it? They say he collapsed in a café just a few hours ago! Such a loss for the literary community."

Cole felt a cold chill run down his spine. "Yes, it's tragic," he said, forcing his voice to remain steady. "He had a sharp tongue, but he was a talent, for sure."

Claire studied him, her gaze piercing. "You knew him well, didn't you? You were always so passionate about your work. Did he ever—"

"—ever review my books?" Ethan finished, a wry smile creeping onto his lips. "More like tear them apart. But that's the nature of this business and that was his nature too. You take the hits and keep going, right? TCB— take care of business, " he said.

She sighed, shaking her head. "It's not right. The way critics can hold so much power over an author's career. It's like they forget we're human."

He felt a strange sense of camaraderie with Claire as if their shared frustration with the literary world could bridge the chasm that had grown between them. But he had to be careful—too much honesty could lead to questions he wasn't ready to answer.

"Exactly," he said, leaning back, a mask of nonchalance in place. "But we do what we must to survive, right? It's really great to see you again!" In the back of his mind he thought it was all good and she could be used as an alibi just in case.

They sat under the trees in the silence for a moment, the weight of unspoken words hanging in the air. Finally, Claire broke the stillness, her voice barely above a whisper. She put her hand on his thigh. "I always admired your talent, Ethan. You have a way of capturing emotions few others can. I hope you find the success you deserve," she said softly. She was flirting and her words felt like a lifeline, tugging at the edges of his heart. He thought about kissing her but he quickly brushed the thought aside, given what had just transpired at the cafe.

"Thanks, Claire. That means a lot to me," he said.

As she turned to leave, Cole felt a pang of guilt twist in his gut. He had just taken a life to protect his own dreams, yet here was someone who genuinely believed in his potential. The contrast felt jarring, but he pushed the feelings aside. He had a lot on his mind and he was giving serious thought to leaving town and going on a trip somewhere.

After Claire walked away, he was left alone once more, the park quieting as the sun fully departed with the evening taking hold. Cole took a deep breath, reminding himself of the rage that had driven him. There was no room for regret now. Reese was gone, and soon, the world would forget him.

As the moon rose in the night sky, the street lights came on, their bright illumination shining on the park below, and Ethan began to write again, the pen moving swiftly across the paper, weaving a narrative that felt increasingly alive. Each word was a step further into his new reality, a world where he was free to craft his stories, his own destiny, unencumbered by the judgments of those who could never understand. And he had to insure that he was seen as having nothing too do with the critic's death.

In the fading twilight, Ethan felt a renewed sense of purpose. He was a creator, a storyteller who would no longer allow anyone to stand in the way of his vision and stories. The pages of his life were his to write, and he would make sure that no one erased his words ever again.

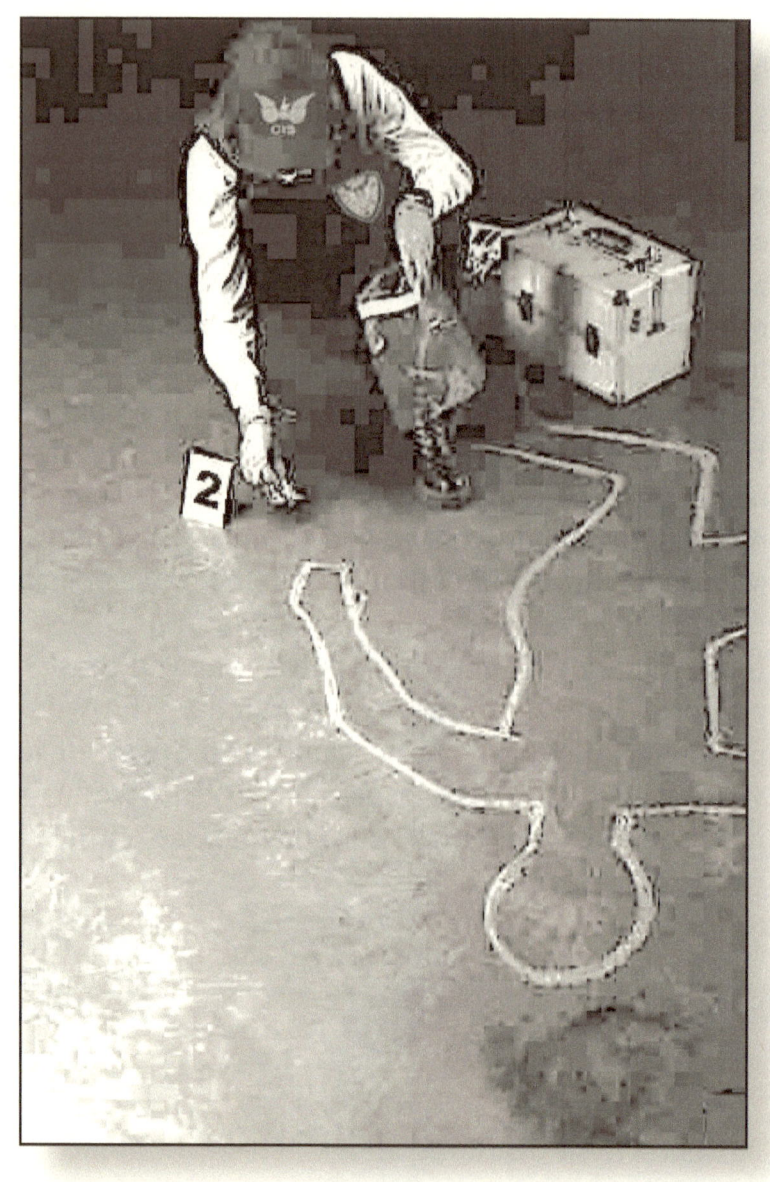

CHAPTER 6

Detecting Detectives
No Stone Left Unturned

A few blocks away from the park, Detective Ava Reynolds stood outside the café, her arms crossed tightly against the chill of the autumn air. She was the #1 local homicide investigator with a future as bright as her eyes. A position she had earned after five years of misogynistic male bullshit. She had learned how to be 'one of the guys' without losing her identity as a woman. Working her way up the PD latter was hard.

Detective Reynolds walked into a room like a storm rolling in, all quiet confidence and sharp edges. Her presence had a gravity to it, pulling every set of eyes toward her without effort or intent. She wasn't just beautiful—she was arresting, the kind of woman you noticed first and regretted later if you missed seeing her. She definitely made a strong impression.

Her hair, dark as espresso and just as smooth, spilled over her shoulders in waves that framed a face carved by contradictions: delicate features sculpted by hardened experience. Her eyes were the kind of blue that could cut glass, piercing through lies like a scalpel. Beneath the crisp collar of her leather jacket, her blouse was as sleek as the lines of her black jeans, an ensemble that whispered style but screamed practicality. She had put up with a lot of BS to get to the top of the heap.

Reynolds's movements were precise and deliberate, like someone who had memorized the art of control and had done this many times before. Her Glock 9mm pistol rested snug in its holster at her hip, a natural extension of her, but it was the way she carried herself that told you she didn't need it to make you regret a bad decision. Her voice, when she spoke, was a low alto—velvet wrapped around steel. Each word she delivered was measured and deliberate, the cadence of someone who had seen too much and still refused to flinch.

She had a mind like a steel trap and a reputation to match—solving cases others had long since written off. But there was something else about her, a shadow in the way her gaze lingered on unsaid things, a hint of vulnerability carefully tucked beneath her armor. Ava Reynolds was gorgeous, yes, but more than that, she was dangerous—because she wasn't afraid to face whatever came her way, even if it meant shining a light on her own dark side.

The police and the Crime Scene Investigation (CSI) team were called because its was a public venue and the death was on an unknown cause. The crime scene was still chaotic; paramedics and CSI hurried in and out, their voices raised in urgent discussions while onlookers whispered in hushed tones, faces drawn with concern. Reynolds took a deep breath, the scent of coffee mingling with the metallic tang of anxiety, and stepped inside, her sharp blue eyes scanning the room.

CSI had just arrived on site. Well known literary critic Calvin Reese lay on the floor of the cafe he frequented often, there was an unsettling stillness around the body now that the frantic rush had subsided. The paramedics had already pronounced him dead at the scene, leaving the small cafe to the police detectives. The Detective stepped over the yellow tape that marked the perimeter of the scene, her heart racing with a familiar mixture of anticipation and dread. This was her job—to unravel the threads of a story that was still freshly woven, and to find the truth buried beneath the surface. How had the victim died and was there any public threat? These were questions that needed answers, ASAP.

She crouched down beside the body, observing the way Calvin's eyes were still open, a look of disbelief etched on his features. It was a face that had often been filled with self-importance, and now, it seemed eerily serene. She noted the half-empty cup of coffee on the table nearby, the slight sheen of sweat still clinging to the victim's forehead.

Detective Reynolds' new partner is Sargent Mark Mills. He's the kind of officer who doesn't blend into the background, no matter how much he tries. Built like a linebacker who'd traded in the turf for the streets, he filled a room with his broad shoulders and quiet, deliberate presence. His uniform was always pressed, boots shined, but there was a rawness to him—like he was just barely keeping the chaos of the crime scene at bay.

His face was a roadmap of long nights and close calls, a sharp jawline peppered with stubble that never quite surrendered to the razor. His nose had a slight crook, a memento from a bar fight in his early years on the force, and his dark brown eyes carried the weight of too many crime scenes. They were the kind of eyes that saw everything—the things most people missed, and the things they wished they could unsee and forget.

Mill's voice was low and gravelly as if it had been worn down by shouting over sirens and long nights at the precinct. He spoke with the pragmatism of someone who knew the rules but wasn't above bending them if it got the job done. His humor was dry, often unexpected, and more of a shield than an invitation. He was easily likable.

On the job, he was relentless, methodical, and unflinching, earning him a reputation as one of the best in homicide. But there was a quiet side to him, one he didn't show often—like when he stared at the tattered photo of his younger brother tucked in his wallet or when he lingered a little too long at the squad room window, coffee growing cold in his hand. Officer Mills wasn't perfect, but he wasn't trying to be. He was just trying to make sense of a world that often didn't, one case at a time. And if he carried a little more of the darkness than he should, well, he figured that was the price he had to pay.

"Detective," called Mills, interrupting her thoughts. He was a rookie, eager but still clumsy in his handling of the crime scene. "We found some witnesses who were here when it happened."

Reynolds stood, brushing off her slacks as she turned her attention to the growing crowd. "Get their statements. I want to know who he was with, what he was doing here and what was said. Find anyone who might have seen anything unusual."

Mills nodded and rushed off, eager to please. She sighed, knowing that a witness list would do little to calm the undercurrent of unease already swirling around the case. She walked over to the café's barista, a young woman with bright pink hair who was still shaking.

"Can you please tell us what happened?" Reynolds asked gently, her tone softening as she noticed the girl's tears and wide frightened eyes.

"I-I was at the register," the barista stammered, clutching a dish towel tightly in her hands. "He's a regular but he was sitting alone, reading a book. Then… then he just started convulsing. I didn't know what to do! I thought he was choking at first, but then…" She trailed off, her voice breaking.

"Did you notice anyone else around him?" Reynolds pressed, jotting down notes in her small notepad.

The girl thought for a moment, her brow furrowed. "There was a man. I didn't see him clearly; he was sitting at the table in the corner, but he got up right after it happened and left."

"Did you get a good look at him… this 'other' guy?" the Detective asked.

"No. I—I was too busy trying to help Mr. Reese," the young waitress said.

"Has anyone else gotten sick?" she asked.

'Not that I know of," said the waitress.

76

Reynolds nodded, trying to piece together the fragments of the incident. A stranger in a café, slipping away after witnessing a man's collapse. Perhaps it was nothing but it was enough to make her uneasy. "What book was he reading?"

The barista's eyes brightened with recognition. "I think it was 'Pages of Death' or something like that... I think I remember seeing the book cover at some point," she said. "It's still on the table."

A chill danced down Reynolds's spine at the title. It seemed too coincidental, and she made a note to bag the book as evidence.

"Thank you. You've been very helpful." As she turned away, she spotted Mills returning with a few more witnesses in tow—two men and a woman, all looking anxious and pale. "Detective," Mills called, gesturing for her to come over.

Reynolds approached, glancing from one face to another. "Can any of you please tell me what happened here today?"

The tallest of the men spoke up first, his voice shaky. "I was sitting over there," he said, pointing to a table near the back window. "I saw the man collapse. It was sudden. One moment he was fine, and the next, he was on the floor."

"Did you see anyone else with him?" The Detective asked, her eyes keen.

The man shook his head. "Nope, he was alone. I didn't notice anything suspicious," he said.

Next the woman, with bright red lipstick and a designer bag, chimed in. "I was at the counter when it happened. He looked unwell before he collapsed. He kept rubbing his chest," she said. "Maybe he had a heart attack?"

"Did he eat or drink anything unusual?" Reynolds pressed, intrigued by the potential for foul play.

"Not that I saw," the woman said. "And his coffee was still warm when the paramedics got here. That's when I noticed the other guy leave."

Reynolds's interest was piqued by this. "Other guy? What did he look like?"

"Just a regular guy," the woman replied. "Dark hair, glasses. He seemed… tense, I guess. I thought he was waiting for someone. I've seen him in here once before," she said.

"Did you see him leave?" the Detective asked.

"Yes. He got up, went over to the guy and I think he said something to him and then he looked around as if he was worried, and then he just hurried our the door and left," she explained.

Reynolds's mind raced. A man had vanished into thin air after witnessing another person collapse?

"Can you describe him further? Anything distinctive?" she asked.

The young woman shook her head, her brow furrowed in concentration. "No, just... average. I didn't think much of it at the time."

"Everyone feeling OK, no one sick?" asked Reynolds.

"We're fine!" they all responded.

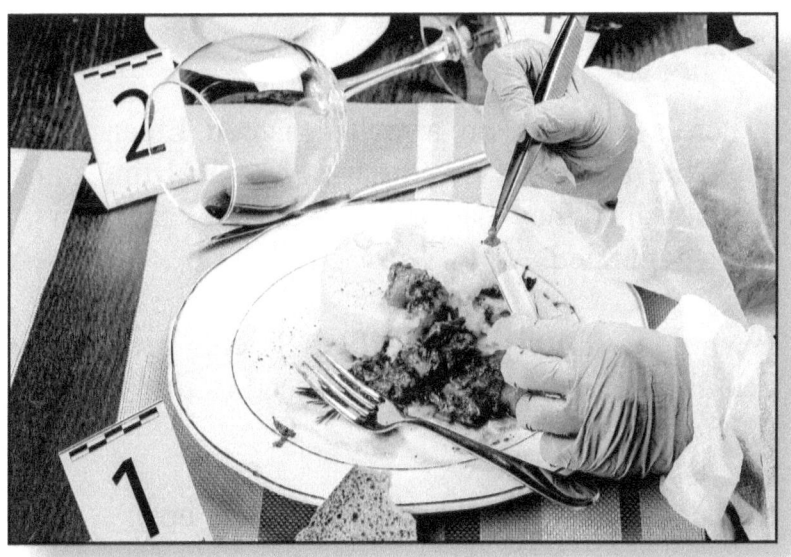

The Detective sighed, frustration mounting. "Alright, thank you very much. You can go but please give Officer Mills here your contact info as we might have some more questions," she said.
As the witnesses dispersed, she glanced back at Reese's sheet-covered body, a gnawing sensation

twisting in her gut. There was something off about this whole situation. The suddenness of the victim's collapse, the mystery man slipping away, and the title of the book—'Death Pages'—it all seemed to taunt her as she sat at the table where Reese had fallen just a few hours before.

"Detective Reynolds," a voice called from behind her. She turned to see Officer Mills approaching, a folder in hand. "I got the background check on Calvin Reese. He's had a few run-ins with disgruntled authors, and there's something else…"

"What?" she asked, curiosity piqued.

"There's a report on a writer named Ethan Cole, someone Reese reviewed harshly several times and it looks like they had a big feud over the years," Mills explained.

Reynolds's interest intensified. "Send me all the details. If Cole is involved, we need to find him and talk to him ASAP."

Mills nodded and scurried off to follow up.

As Reynolds and her team took one last look at the café, she felt the pieces of the puzzle beginning to fit together, but there were still too many unknowns. But one thing was clear…there was more to this than just a natural death! Someone had set this tragedy in motion, and as she dug deeper into critic Calvin Reese's life, she knew she would find the answers lurking in the shadows. Eventually. No one got away with murder on her watch.

After a few more hours processing the crime scene she stepped outside once more, determination flooding her veins. She would uncover the truth, no matter where it led her. The question that loomed in her mind was whether the truth would reveal a killer, or merely a man who had finally met his maker naturally. Either way, the hunt for the whole truth and nothing but the truth, was on.

Metro Police Detective Ava Reynolds parked her car outside the modest brick building that housed Ethan Cole's small publishing office. The late afternoon sun cast a warm glow over the street, but the shadows in her mind remained dark. She glanced at the notes scattered across the passenger seat— Calvin Reese's autopsy report, witness statements, and the background information on Ethan Cole. A picture of the author sat in the middle, his rugged handsomeness overshadowed by a long history of frustration with the literary establishment. Cole had been identified as the man in the Cafe that evening. It was clear from his previous interactions with Reese that they were more than just acquaintances and that there had been more than just a long-standing professional rivalry.

She took a deep breath and stepped out of the car, her high heels clicking on the pavement as she made her way toward the entrance. The building had seen better days, with chipped paint and a flickering light above the door, but a small plaque next to the entrance proclaimed it as the home of Cole Publishing. She pushed the door open, and the faint chime of a bell announced her arrival.

Inside, the space was cluttered but cozy. Shelves lined the walls, filled with books, some new and others yellowing with age. A small desk in the corner held a mountain of papers and a laptop surrounded by empty coffee cups, giving the impression of a writer deeply immersed in their work. Reynolds's eyes roamed the room until she spotted Ethan in the back, pacing in front of a whiteboard filled with hastily scrawled notes, ideas and character sketches.

"Ethan Cole?" she called out, her voice echoing slightly in the quiet room.

He turned, his expression shifting from surprise to guarded interest. "Yep, that's me. Can I help you?"

She stepped forward, her badge visible as she held it up. "Detective Reynolds, with the police. I'd like to ask you a few questions about Calvin Reese."

His posture stiffened, and the faint flicker of wariness in his eyes didn't go unnoticed. "What about him?"

"Are you aware he collapsed earlier today? He died at the scene," she said, watching his reaction closely.

For a moment, Ethan seemed taken aback, his mouth opening slightly as if the words hadn't registered. Then he recovered quickly, a flicker of something—regret or perhaps relief—passing across his face. "I didn't know. I hadn't heard anything. It's tragic. He was a brilliant critic and a wonderful guy."

She studied him, looking for any hint of deception. "You had a public disagreement with him for a long time did you not?"

Ethan's eyes narrowed, and his jaw tightened. "We had a few exchanges before, yes. He didn't hold back his opinions about my work, but that's part of being an author. We knew each other back in Grad School too," he said. "Most writers hated him then too but he seemed to relish in it."

"Did it bother you that he was always so harsh in his reviews about your work?" Reynolds probed, trying to gauge his emotional response. "That had to hurt your ego a bit, didn't it?"

"Of course," Cole replied, his tone turning defensive. "But we understand that it's not personal. It's business. Critics have a job to do. He was an arrogant ass but I never wished him harm."

Reynolds stepped closer, her voice dropping to a more intimate tone. "Where were you around yesterday evening, Mr. Cole?"

"Yes, I was here, working," he said, his gaze shifting to the floor as if the weight of her question pressed on him. "I didn't leave the office until later." (That of course, was a lie as he was writing in the park about 2 blocks from the cafe,)

"Is there anyone that can vouch for your whereabouts?" she asked.

Cole hesitated, the tension in the air thickening. "I was alone, but I can show you my work log. I was focused on my latest book, trying to meet a deadline," he explained.

Reynolds noted his defensiveness but also the sincerity in his eyes. "I'll need to see that log, along with any correspondence you've had with Calvin Reese recently. If there's anything else, anything at all, I suggest you tell me now because tomorrow might be too late. We are trying to clear you and move forward with the investigation," she said.

He nodded, the lines on his forehead deepening. "Fine. I'll get it for you."

As Cole turned to retrieve the documents, Reynolds took a moment to observe the room more closely. The walls were plastered with posters of book covers and literary events nd awards, but one poster caught her attention—a promotional piece for a writer's festival featuring both Ethan Cole and Calvin Reese. The two men stood together in the picture, both smiling, yet the tension between them was palpable even through the glossy poster.

Ethan returned with a stack of papers, his expression neutral, though Ava could see the tension in his shoulders. "Here's my log and some emails I exchanged with Calvin. You'll see they were mostly professional," he said.

The Detective leafed through the papers, noting the lack of warmth in the emails, the sharpness of Reese's critiques hanging in the air like a blade. "You were frustrated with him, yes?" she asked.

Coles's lips pressed into a thin line. "More than anything, I was annoyed. I'm an author who wants to be taken seriously, and Mr. Reese was making a career out of belittling my work. It's hard to stomach when you put your heart into what you create and it was clear to me and everyone in the community that he had it in for me!"

"Is that why you decided to meet him today?" Reynolds asked, probing deeper. "Did you think you could confront him about all this?"

"No, not at all" Ethan replied quickly, perhaps too quickly. "I had no intention of meeting him then or at any time. I only found out he was at the café because I was passing by and stopped in for a cup on coffee. Pure coincidence," he said.

"You planning to talk to him at all?" she inquired.

He hesitated again, the weight of the question hanging in the air. "I thought about it, but I decided against it. I didn't like him and he didn't like me nor my work," he said.

"Were you at the Cafe? And if so why?" Reynolds pressed.

Cole glanced away, the facade of confidence wavering for a brief moment. "As I said before... I often go there to work. It's a nice place for inspiration. A man can still have a cup of java in this town, can't he?" he asked defensively.

The Detective nodded but sensed that there was more to this story. "You understand that with his death, you're now a person of interest in this investigation? Any unresolved issues you had with him might raise eyebrows. You should tell me now," she said.

Cole's eyes flashed with indignation. "There's nothing to tell. This is absurd! I didn't kill him! I barely knew the man personally. We were professional acquaintances at best," he said adamantly.

"Acquaintances who exchanged some pretty harsh words over the years, and now he's dead," she said, her voice steady. "And someone saw you say something to him right before leaving the café and right after he collapsed!"

"What?" Cole's expression turned from indignation to disbelief. "That's impossible. I didn't see anyone. I was too busy working."

"People don't just collapse and die without cause, Mr. . .... Cole," Ava countered, leaning forward. "And the witnesses mentioned that someone saw a man leave just after the incident. That man fits your description. That man is you!" she said.

Ethan's expression hardened, and he crossed his arms. "I didn't kill him. If you want to accuse me of something, you'll need more than mere speculation. I want a lawyer!"

Reynolds studied him, assessing the flicker of anger and fear in his eyes. "I don't want to accuse you of anything, sir. We just want the truth," she said. "But you need to understand how serious this is. If you have any information that could help us clear your name or lead us to the truth, now would be the time to share it," she said. "You're in a world of hurt."

Cole seemed to wrestle with his thoughts, the tension palpable. After a long silence, he spoke, his voice barely above a whisper. "In my notebook, you will see that... I had an idea for a story about a critic who meets a tragic end. But it was just a story idea... I never intended for all this to become a reality. I swear," Cole said.

The words hung in the air, laden with implications. The Detective's mind raced at the prospect of an author's imagination intertwining with real life, but she couldn't let herself be swayed by the emotional weight of his pseudo-confession.

"Stories have a way of reflecting the truth, Ethan," she said slowly. "May I call you Ethan?" She asked. "Sure," he responded with a handsome smile. "I think I would like that."

The next day Detective Ava Reynolds stood at the cork board in her cluttered office at the 10th Precinct, staring at the grainy photograph pinned in the center. A single spotlight above her flickered, casting uneasy shadows on the walls. The image showed the café where Calvin Reese had spent his last night alive—a small, cozy place called The Old Village Cafe. The photograph, taken from the café's exterior security camera, showed a man seated near the window, his back to the lens.

"You really think this is going to lead somewhere?" Officer Mills asked skeptically as he leaned against the doorframe.

Reynolds didn't answer immediately. Instead, she gestured to the image, where the faint outline of a hand rested on the table. "Look at this…" holding a magnifying glass up to the 8x10 B&W photo.

Mills stepped closer, squinting at the picture. "It's just a blurry handprint. What are you hoping to get out of that?"

"A fingerprint," Reynolds said, her voice steady, almost daring him to doubt her.

He blinked at her, incredulous. "From this? Come on, Ava. This photo's trash! You can barely make out the guy's shape, let alone get a finger print. It has never been done before."

"Maybe," Reynolds said. "But the wiz's in the crime lab tell me it can be done, besides it's all we've got. Ethan Cole swears he wasn't there that night, but if we can place him at this table, his alibi falls apart."

Mills folded his arms, the skepticism wavering. "And how do you propose we do that? Magic?"

"Not magic," she said, "Technology!" grabbing the photograph and pinning it to a light box on the desk. "I sent this to the lab earlier, had them enhance and enlarge it as much as possible. They sent back a high-res version."

He slid a manila envelope across the desk, and Mills pulled out the newly printed image. The hand was much sharper now, the faint ridges of what could be fingerprints just visible.

"That's… impressive," she admitted, though her tone still held a hint of doubt. "But even if those are fingerprints, how are you planning to lift them? It's a photograph, not a crime scene."

Reynolds smirked. "That's where it gets verrrrrry interesting."

She opened another drawer and pulled out a portable digital scanner, setting it next to the light box. "This little gadget scans high-resolution images for patterns—fingerprint ridges, shoe treads, you name it. If there's a clear enough print here, the scanner

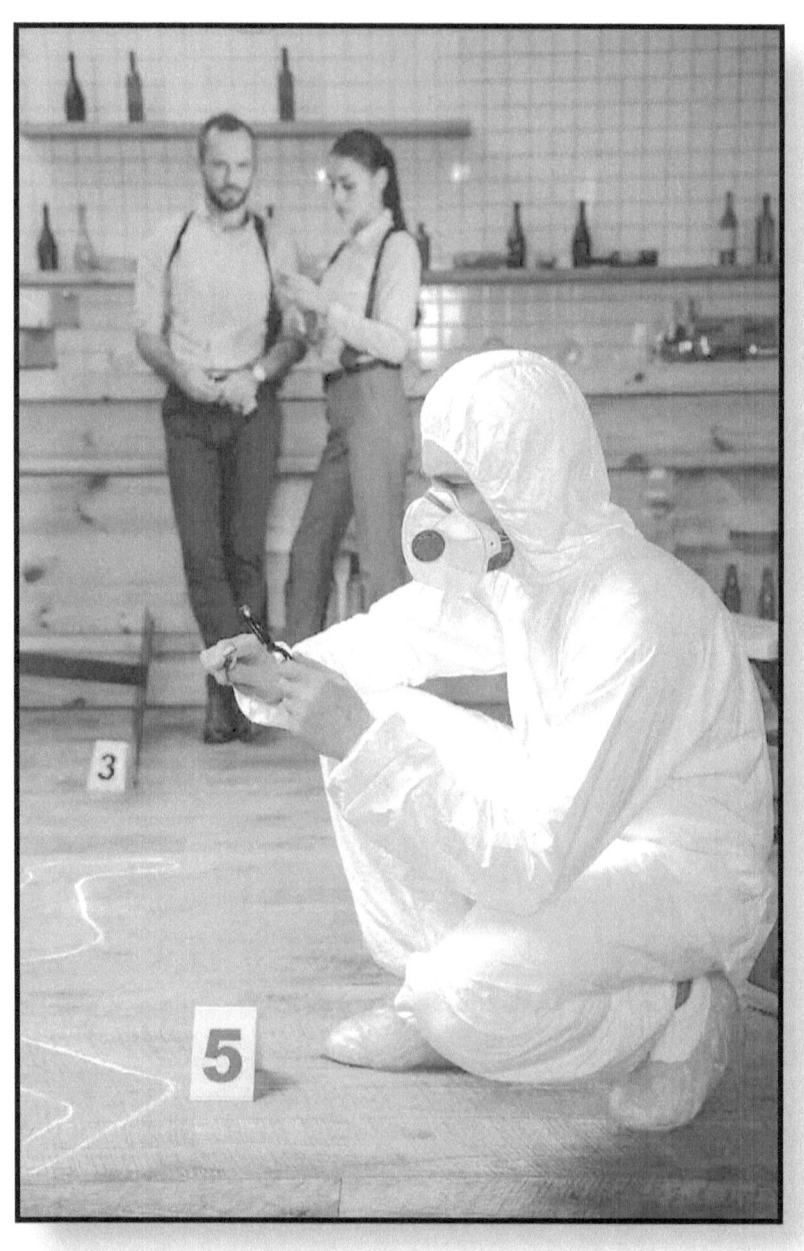

will pick it up and convert it into something we can run through the Local, State Police and FBI databases."

Mills leaned in his curiosity finally piqued. "Does it actually work?"

"We're about to find out!" she said.

Reynolds powered up the scanner, its soft hum filling the room as she carefully positioned the enhanced photo beneath it. Mills watched in silence as the machine's light swept over the image, line by line, capturing every detail.

Minutes passed. Finally, the scanner beeped. A small window on the accompanying laptop displayed a loading bar as it processed the scanned data.

"Okay," Reynolds said, her voice tight with anticipation. "Let's see what we've got."

The screen blinked, and a magnified version of the finger print appeared, with one section highlighted in green. Reynolds zoomed in further. The ridges of a fingerprint were now unmistakable.

"You've got to be kidding me," Mills murmured, leaning in closer. "That's an actual print!"

"Looks like it," Reynolds said, trying to suppress the surge of triumph in her chest. "Now let's see if it matches anything."

She loaded the digital print into the department's database, initiating a cross-check with the interagency records database. If they had ever been finger printed they would be found. The process was agonizingly slow, each passing second stretching into what seemed like an eternity. Mills paced behind her, the rhythmic click of his boots the only sound in the room.

Finally, the computer dinged. A match popped up on the screen, accompanied by a mugshot.

"Ethan Cole," Mills said, reading the name aloud.
Reynolds exhaled sharply. "There it is. Proof Cole was in the Old Village the night Reese was killed."
Mills studied the screen, his initial doubt replaced by something resembling admiration. "That's some solid work, Detective. But it's circumstantial, isn't it? Just because he was in the café doesn't mean he killed Reese."

"It doesn't," Reynolds agreed, already gathering the files. "But it destroys his alibi and he lied to me. I don't like that! He said he wasn't anywhere near Reese that night. Now we know that's a lie."

Mills nodded, his expression hardening. "And if he's lying about that, what else is he hiding?"

Reynolds got her coat. "Exactly... let's go find out."
The next morning, Ethan Cole sat across from Reynolds and Mills in the cramped interrogation

room, his usual calm demeanor beginning to show some cracks.

"You've been adamant, Mr. Cole," Reynolds said, his voice measured, "that you weren't anywhere near the Old Village Cafe on the night of Calvin Reese's murder."

"That's right," Cole replied, his tone clipped.

Reynolds slid the enhanced photograph across the table. "Care to explain this?"

He glanced at the photo, his brow furrowing slightly, but he said nothing.

"See that hand on the table?" Reynolds continued, pointing to the image. "That's yours. We lifted your fingerprint from this photo, and it's an exact match." Ethan's jaw tightened, but he didn't respond.

"This is your chance, Cole," Mills said, leaning forward. "Tell us the truth. What were you doing there that night?"

For a moment, Cole said nothing. Then he leaned back in his chair, his eyes dark and unreadable.
"I was at the café," he admitted finally, his voice quiet. "But I didn't kill Calvin."
Reynolds exchanged a quick glance with Mills.

"Then why lie about it?" Reynolds pressed.

"Because I knew how it would look," Cole said, his voice rising slightly. "I argued with Reese online all the time. We fought. It wasn't pretty. But I didn't kill him. When I left the café, he was still alive."

"Convenient story," Mills said, his tone sharp.

"It's the truth," Cole snapped, his composure slipping further.

Reynolds leaned forward, her gaze piercing. "The truth, Mr. Cole, is that you lied and your fingerprints now place you at the scene. The truth is that Calvin Reese was found dead just minutes after you were seen there. And the truth is that every lie you tell only makes you look guiltier," the Detective said.

Cole's fists clenched on the table, but he didn't respond.

"Ethan you need to tread carefully and you need to see an Attorney. I'll be in touch," she said.

As silence filled the room, Reynolds felt the shift in the air. The case was far from closed, but for the first time, they had Ethan Cole on the defensive. And that, Reynolds thought, was a good start

As she turned to leave, the young Detective felt a mixture of intrigue and unease. Ethan Cole was a man caught between his ambitions and the shadow of a critic. Had Reese pushed Cole too far? In the dance between fiction and reality, who was the true author of Calvin Reese's murder? For some reason she did not want to believe it was Cole but the evidence, circumstantial though it may be, was mounting against him.

As the door swung shut behind her, Reynolds couldn't shake the feeling that they were just scratching the surface of a deeper story—a narrative where ambition, jealousy, and murder collided in a deadly game of words and best sellers. She had to dig deeper. She had to find out who was truly pulling the strings before someone else paid the price for another story gone wrong. But since when could a book be used as a weapon of murder?

Ethan Cole adjusted the stiff, black wig perched uncomfortably on his head and pulled the brim of the fedora lower over his eyes. The tinted glasses helped, but he couldn't shake the feeling that every mourner in the room could see straight through his disguise. A too-tight black suit completed the charade—borrowed from a thrift store and smelling faintly of mothballs. Cole glanced around the packed funeral home, doing his best to blend in among the somber faces.

Calvin Reese. The name still burned in Ethan's mind. Not just a critic, but his critic—the man who had torn apart every novel Ethan had published over the past decade. Reese hadn't just reviewed books; he dissected them, eviscerated them with glee, and then salted the earth. And yet, here Ethan was, standing among Reese's friends and family, pretending to pay respects to a man he'd fantasized about strangling with his own typewriter ribbon.

Why? Because Calvin Reese's death wasn't natural, Cole knew it and so did anyone there. The obituaries had said Calvin died of a heart attack, collapsing in a local Cafe just a week after publishing another scathing takedown—this time of a debut novel that had received rave reviews everywhere else. Calvin Reese didn't just die. Calvin Reese killed—at least in the literary sense.

And then there was the letter. It had arrived shortly thereafter at the 10th Precinct addressed to 'Detective Ava Reynolds', unsigned and cryptic: *"Sometimes even critics write their own obituaries. Watch the funeral. You'll know what to do."* She didn't know what to make of it. But by the time the obituary ran in the paper the next day, he'd fished it out again, smoothing the paper and read the words until they blurred.

And now here was Cole, sweating under someone else's hairpiece, pretending to grieve a man he publicly and openly loathed.

The funeral parlor smelled of lilies and furniture polish. A mahogany coffin rested at the front, surrounded by an extravagant spray of white roses. Ethan took a seat in the back row, close enough to observe but far enough to avoid awkward small talk. The assemblage quieted itself and the eulogy began.

"He was a man of many words," said the officiant, a thin, balding man who sounded like he'd swallowed a thesaurus. "His pen was his sword, his shield, and sometimes his undoing. He was a special and giving man. A truly nice person," he said. It was quite obvious the man had never met Calvin Reese.

Ethan smirked despite himself. That was one way to describe a man whose reviews were better known than the books they critiqued. But he kept his head bowed, feigning the solemnity that such an occasion demanded.

The crowd was small—smaller than Ethan had expected for someone of Reese's notoriety. A smattering of faces he recognized: a few rival critics, authors Calvin had once championed, and a handful of publishing bigwigs who probably owed him favors. But one face caught Cole's attention—a woman sitting in the second row, her veil thick and black, obscuring her features. She sat stiffly, hands clasped over a small black purse.

Ethan didn't know her, but something about her posture, her stillness, felt wrong.

The officiant finished his speech, and the mourners began to rise, one by one, to share their memories of Calvin. Most were polite, generic—words like "brilliant," "uncompromising," and "larger-than-life" and other BS floated through the air.
Then the woman in the black veil stood.

She moved with purpose, stepping to the podium and lowering her veil as she turned to face the room. Her face was striking—sharp cheekbones, deep-set eyes, and lips painted a shade too bright for the occasion. She held the room in a silence that stretched longer than was comfortable.

"Good Afternoon, my name is Lila March," she began, her voice smooth and low. "I was Mr. Reese's assistant."

Ethan sat up straight. He'd never heard of her.

"I worked with Calvin for five years," she continued. "And in those years, I learned that the man behind the words was... complicated."

A polite cough rippled through the crowd.

"Calvin had enemies," Lila said, her voice growing sharper. "But he had friends too. He also had secrets. And those secrets didn't die with him."

A ripple of unease moved through the room. Ethan's pulse quickened.

Lila reached into her purse and pulled out a slim envelope. "I found this in Calvin's desk," she said. "A letter he wrote right before he died. A letter meant for someone... in this room."

Ethan clenched his fists. Lila opened the envelope and began to read:

"To the one who finds this—
If you're reading these words, it means I've finally met my match. But don't mourn me. Instead, avenge me! My killer is here, among the mourners, hiding in

*plain sight. Look closely, and you'll see the truth.
C"*

Gasps and murmurs filled the room.

Cole froze, the words pounding in his ears.

Lila folded the letter and slid it back into the envelope. "Whoever you are," she said, her eyes scanning the crowd, "Calvin knew you. And he knew you'd come. You'll be caught and you'll pay!"

The tension in the room was palpable. Cole felt his disguise slip, his hand instinctively tugging at the brim of his hat. Lila's gaze swept over the crowd lingering on him for a heartbeat, and then moving on. The funeral ended in a murmur of speculation. The mourners filed out in twos and threes, exchanging whispers and sideways glances.Cole lingered near the back, his mind racing.

And the question in everyone's mind now was 'who killed Calvin Reese?' And why had the killer come here, risking exposure? Cole was asking himself just about the same thing.

As the room emptied, he noticed Lila standing near the coffin, speaking in hushed tones to a man in a dark suit. Cole approached, his feet moving before his brain could object.

"Excuse me," he said, keeping his voice low and steady. "Ms. March?"

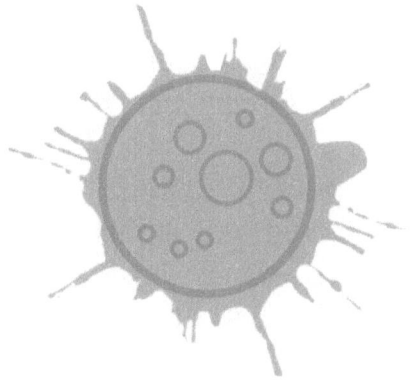

She turned, her eyes sharp and assessing. "Yes?"

"I couldn't help but hear what you said earlier," Cole said. "About the letter…"

Her lips twitched into a faint smile. "And you are?"
"Martin," Cole lied. "A… friend of Calvin's."

"Martin." She said his name slowly, almost tasting it. "Well, Martin, Calvin didn't have many friends. And in the end I think his past caught up with him."

"Ya know I was thinking the exact same thing!" Cole said, subtly touching her elbow in a sensuous kind of way, "Can I buy you a drink?" The two left together arm and arm shortly thereafter and were not seen the rest of the afternoon.
Later Detective Ana Reynolds tightened her trench coat against the chill as she stood outside the Farmington Hills Funeral Home. The rain had

stopped hours ago, but the damp air and grey skies lingered, clinging to a somber atmosphere. Calvin Reese's funeral just happened yet his death refuses to be buried with him. Initially ruled a heart attack, the autopsy and the toxicology report had now revealed a whole different story: poisoning.

The toxin was exotic—Tetraxin, is precise and lethal and it is engineered not naturally occurring. It wasn't the sort of thing someone just stumbled across. No, whoever had killed Reese had planned it meticulously. They'd chosen a public Cafe as the stage for the murder and it appeared the killer had mixed the poison into something Reese had consumed there. The timing was yet to be established. If poison is ingested in the right amount it would ensured the victim died shortly thereafter, hopefully far from the scene, muddying the trail.

The investigation had no way of knowing that Reese had been sick for a day or two before goin in for his bi-weekly cup of cappuccino.

Now it was Reynolds' job to untangle the knots. Her first lead was simple: All the people in the Cafe that evening and all the people who had attended Reese's funeral. His killer would have been in one or both places. Rage and hubris had brought them together

The young detective pushed through the doors of the funeral home and approached the front desk.

"Detective Reynolds," she said, flashing her badge. "I need the guestbook from Calvin Reese's funeral."

The funeral director, a thin man with a nervous energy, hesitated. "Gee Detective, I don't know if I can— Don't you need a warrant?"

"Mr. Ashcroft," she interrupted. "A man was poisoned and I'm on track to catch his killer! You can either help me now or explain your delay to the district attorney later. Your choice."

Ashcroft blanched, then scurried off. Moments later, he returned with the guestbook, its leather cover polished and pristine.

"Thank you," she said, taking the book. She flipped through its pages, scanning the names. Some names she recognized from her research: writers Calvin had eviscerated in his reviews, publishing executives whose livelihoods he had threatened, and a handful of other critics who had both admired and feared him. One name stood out—Lila March, Calvin's assistant, who had delivered a cryptic eulogy about secrets and enemies. Reynolds circled her name.

"Let me know if you remember anything unusual," she told Ashcroft, snapping the book shut. "I'll be in touch."

Reese's assistant Lila March lived in an upscale high-rise that oozed money and taste. When Reynolds knocked on the door, it opened to reveal a woman as polished as her surroundings. March's jet-black hair was pulled into a tight chignon, her crimson lipstick and eye makeup was flawless. She was wearing a $3000 tailored Giorgio Armani outfit, as though expecting a fashion magazine shoot rather than a police visit.

"Detective Reynolds," March said, her voice smooth. "I was wondering when you'd show up."
"You don't seem very surprised," said Reynolds.

March stepped aside to let her in. The apartment was immaculate, with floor-to-ceiling windows offering a wonderful view of the city. Bookshelves lined one wall, stacked with first editions and signed copies. A single wineglass rested on the coffee table, its contents untouched.

"I know Calvin's death wasn't natural," March started, gesturing for Reynolds to sit. "And it's just like him to make a spectacle even from the grave!"

Reynolds remained standing. "Tell me about the cafe. Did you meet him there that day?"

March's eyes narrowed slightly, but her composure didn't falter. "No. But I know he went there often. He liked to conduct business in neutral spaces. It made people feel comfortable. Of course, he wasn't meeting me that day. He didn't need to."

"What kind of business?" the Detective asked.

March leaned back against the couch, her fingers idly tracing the edge of her wineglass. "Calvin collected secrets, Detective. He had files on everyone—writers, editors, other critics, even the staff at publishing houses. He knew their vices, their mistakes, their weaknesses. And he used that knowledge to maintain and enhance his power."

"Blackmail?" she asked.

March's smile was cold. "I didn't say that."

Reynolds feverishly jotted notes down in her pad. "You attended the funeral. Why?"

March's tone sharpened. "Because, despite his flaws, I worked for him for five years. He was brilliant and cruel in equal measure. But he gave me my start in this industry and I was grateful."

Reynolds studied her. March's answers were direct and precise, almost rehearsed.

"Do you own a pair of dark sunglasses?" The Detective asked suddenly.

March's eyes flicked up, startled, "Yes. Why?"

"The staff at the Cafe said Mr. . .... Reese was meeting a woman wearing sunglasses that day."

March crossed her arms. "Well, it wasn't me I can tell you that. And I'm sure there are plenty of women with sunglasses in this city."

Reynolds didn't press further. She had a feeling she would be circling back to March soon enough.

Michael Hawthorne's was a suspect with a townhouse that was a stark contrast to March's apartment. Books and papers were scattered across every available surface, the air thick with the smell of stale coffee, bourbon and neglect.

"Detective," Hawthorne said, his voice a low grumble as he ushered Reynolds inside. His disheveled appearance and bloodshot eyes spoke volumes. "Common in, I just got up," he said as the clock behind him read 3pm.

"You attended Calvin Reese's funeral correct," Reynolds said without preamble. "Why?"

Hawthorne poured himself a large Martini— with two olives and downed it before answering.

"To make sure he was really dead!" he said with a smirk.

"Did you have any contact with him recently?"

Hawthorne slammed the glass onto the table, his bitterness palpable. "No! The last time I spoke to that asshole was five years ago, after he almost destroyed my career."

"Destroyed how?" Reynolds asked.

"In almost every way that matters to me," he said.
Then Hawthorne laughed bitterly. "He called my book 'a bloated exercise in narcissism.' And said that it was 'literary masturbation'! That review killed my sales, my publisher dropped me, and then my agent stopped returning my calls. He destroyed my life and Detective I'm glad he's dead!"

"Did you see him at the cafe that day," she inquired. Hawthorne's expression darkened. "No. But if I had, believe me, I wouldn't have wasted poison on him. I'd have killed him with my bare hands!"

His anger seemed genuine and Reynolds felt that at this point, she couldn't rule him out.

Next on the Detective's interview list was Rebecca Porter. With a home that was pristine and a vision of suburban perfection, Porter was petite and cheerful. But from the first Reynolds noticed the tremor in her hands as she poured tea.

"You've had a difficult relationship with Calvin Reese for a long time, isn't that true?" she began.

Porter nodded, her expression tight. "Yes. His review of my debut novel was devastating. But it also pushed me to improve. I owe my success to him in a strange way," Porter said.

"Do you own any sunglasses?" asked Reynolds.
Rebecca hesitated, her smile faltering. "Yes of course they're over there but... what does that have to do with anything?"

"The Cafe staff described the person Mr. Reese was meeting as a woman in sunglasses. Were you there?" Porter's teacup rattled as she set it down. "No. I wasn't." Her denial came too fast, too forced and the Detective made a note to verify Porter's alibi.

By the time Reynolds returned to her desk back at the 10th, her notebook was filled with a dozen contradictions and suspicions. March's cryptic comments, Hawthorne's open hatred, and Porter's nervous denials all pointed in different directions. But one detail tied them together: the Cafe. Reynolds dialed the store manager again. "Can you remember anything else about the woman Calvin met that night?" she prodded. There was a pause before the manager replied. "She was wearing red lipstick. That stood out."

Reynold's mind immediately returned to Lila March and her signature crimson lips.
Grabbing her coat, Reynold's left for a second trip to March's apartment. When she knocked, there was no answer. She called out, her voice echoing in the

hallway. "Lila March, this is Detective Reynolds. Please open the door." No response. The young police Detective pressed her ear to the door and heard faint shuffling. Her instincts kicked in. Drawing her weapon, she kicked the door open. The apartment was empty, Porter was no where to be found. The back window and patio sliding glass door was wide open, curtains billowing in the breeze. On the coffee table sat a red lipstick tube and a folded note. Reynolds picked it up, her pulse racing…

Yo Detective,
You're close, but not close enough.
See ya soon!
Your Killer

The signature was the print of a single crimson kiss.

CHAPTER 7

A Perfect Crime?
Getting Away with Murder

The following morning, Detective Ava Reynolds settled into her usual cubical at the 10th, her desk cluttered with crime files, photos, and notes. Outside the window, the streets of the city happily buzzed with life, but inside, an undercurrent of tension simmered as she rifled through the latest autopsy reports on Calvin Reese's death. The investigation was far from straightforward, and with each piece of evidence she uncovered, a new layer of complexity emerged and Cole's guilt grew. For every question they answered, two more popped up.

The precinct building was a relic, stubbornly standing on the corner of an overgrown block where the city forgot its promises of revitalization. Its brick façade, once red as fresh blood, had faded into a patchy brown, stained by decades of soot and rain. The windows, barred and begrimed, reflected only shadows, and like the precinct had secrets to keep even from itself.

Inside, the air was heavy with the tang of old coffee, stale cigarettes, and a faint undercurrent of sweat and gun oil. Fluorescent lights flickered in uneven intervals, casting pools of pale light on cracked linoleum floors and peeling walls. Desks, older than the beat cops who sat at them, were scarred with carvings, cigarette burns, and dents that whispered of angry fists and frustrated nights.

The bullpen was a chaotic symphony of clattering keyboards, ringing phones, and the occasional bark of an overworked sergeant. Yellowing case files spilled out of filing cabinets like confessions too urgent to contain, while a cork board on the far wall groaned under the weight of thumbtacked photos, newspaper clippings, and string connecting them like arteries to a heart that had long stopped beating.

In the corner, a single wooden chair sat beside an interrogation table, its surface gouged with knife marks and cigarette burns. Above it, a single bare bulb swung lazily on its cord, its dim light barely reaching the stained ceiling tiles. The holding cells beyond the bullpen reeked of sweat and despair, their rusted bars screaming every time they were slid open or slammed shut.

This was a precinct where justice wasn't blind—it just squinted, muttered, and cut corners. Where the line between cop and criminal blurred in the late hours, and everyone had a story they wished they hadn't lived or at least remembered.

Reynolds's phone buzzed, snapping her out of her thoughts. It was Officer Mills, his voice crackling through the speaker. "Detective, I've got something you need to see."

"Go ahead," she replied, straightening in her chair. "We just received the toxicology report from the medical examiner's lab. It's... well, you need to see it for yourself."

"On my way," she responded.

She grabbed her coat and headed down the hall, the sound of her heels echoing against the black and white tile floor. The bustling precinct faded as she entered the sterile environment of the forensic lab, the smell of antiseptic sharp in the air. Mills was waiting for her, his brow furrowed with concern.

"What'd ya find?" she asked, her voice urgent.

Mills handed her a folder, and she opened it, her heart racing as she scanned the contents. The report, which took twice as long as normal to produce, detailed the presence of a very rare poison—one that was known for its untraceable, delayed, but deadly effects. It was a compound derived from an African plant known as 'Aconitum', often referred to as 'Wolfsbane' or 'Monkshood'. She had heard of it once before and the very mention of it sent chills through the young Detective and as well as the Medical Examiner.

"Holy hell," she breathed, looking up at Mills. "This isn't just an accident or a heart attack. Someone killed this guy!"

"Exactly," Mills said, leaning in closer. "And there's more. The poison can be easily extracted and then applied to surfaces—like the pages of a book!"

They looked at each other and Reynolds' mind raced back to Ethan Cole's words. "He was reading 'Death Pages' at the café. If someone had access to that book, they could easily apply the poison to it and leave almost no trace. Can it dry that rapidly? And because this poison is so rare the ME would have to be specifically looking for it," she said as she thought aloud to herself.

"Do you think Cole had something to do with this?" Mills asked, the uncertainty clear in his tone.

The Detective considered this for a long moment... "He does have motive, that's for sure. But he was adamant he didn't want to confront or even meet Reese. Plus, there's the timeline. He claims to have been working during the time of the incident and he has an alibi."

Mills nodded, his expression contemplative. "Maybe we should look into anyone else who might have had access to that book—friends even other authors who could've been at that café before."

"Yes," Reynolds agreed; her instincts were telling her that this was more complicated than a simple rivalry. "Let's dig into Reese's recent interactions. Who else did he review? Who did he meet with? Who else hated him? I want to find out who might have felt similarly betrayed and who had a motive. Standard SOP, let's go down the list," she said.

Mills took note, his pen scratching against his notepad. "I'll pull all of Reese's review history and cross-reference it with anyone who might have had a reason to want him gone," he said.

Reynolds left the lab, her mind churning with thoughts. She couldn't shake the feeling that they were on the brink of discovering something significant. The rare poison indicated a level of premeditated planning that went beyond simple revenge; it hinted at something darker and premeditated. It was a web of connections between authors, critics, and the treachery that lurked in the world of today's literature.

Back at her precinct desk, Reynolds booted up her computer and began searching for Calvin Reese's recently published reviews. As she sifted through articles, BLOGs and online posts, a pattern began to emerge. Reese had not only criticized Ethan Cole's work but had also penned scathing critiques of several other authors, some of whom had made their careers from his approval or disapproval. He seemed to have made a career out of tearing apart the books of local authors.

One name jumped out at her—Margot Lanes, an up-and-coming novelist whose debut had received a glowing review from Reese but had turned sour with his subsequent critiques. Margot had written about personal struggles, and Reese had called her latest work "a meandering journey through self-pity."

Reynolds felt a sense of urgency. It was time to pay Ms Lanes a visit. If she had been humiliated by Reese she had motive and there was a chance she could have snapped.

"Hey, Mills!" she called across the squad room, her voice filled with determination.

"Yeah?" he replied, looking up from his notes.

"Find Margot Lanes. I want to speak with her about her relationship with Calvin Reese. She might be able to shed light on more than just her work."

Mills nodded, his eyes focused. "I'm on it."

As Reynolds stepped out into the crisp fall air, she felt a mix of anticipation and anxiety. The evidence was mounting, and the further she dug, the clearer it became that the literary world was fraught with jealousy, ambition, and betrayal. Each author's ambition intertwined with their fears of being judged, creating a volatile mixture.

She arrived at a quaint coffee spot Margot Lanes was known to frequent, her mind racing with questions. The café was filled with the aroma of fresh brews and the low hum of conversation. Reynolds scanned the room until she spotted the young author sitting at a table by the window, her dark hair falling in loose waves around her shoulders, her face drawn with concern.

"Ms. Lanes?" she approached, her badge and ID visible as she introduced herself. "I'm Detective Reynolds from the local police. May I join you?"

Margot Lanes looked up, surprise flashing in her hazel eyes before she nodded, pulling her laptop close. "Sure. What's this all about?"

Margot Lanes wasn't the type of woman you'd expect to be accused of murder. On the surface, she was all softness and charm, the kind of local celebrity who hosted book club events and signed novels at the quaint bookstore downtown. But under that polished exterior, there was something else— something that didn't sit right with the neighbors now that Calvin Reese was dead.

She had the look of an author who belonged on her own dust jacket: tall, with auburn hair swept into a loose bun that always seemed perfectly imperfect. Her wardrobe was a mix of cozy knit sweaters and bohemian scarves, the kind of aesthetic that screamed literary sophistication. Her honey-brown eyes, framed by delicate glasses, seemed warm at first glance, but if you looked closer, they carried a sharpness, a weight, as if they were always writing stories about the people around her.

Margot had made her name with slow-burn psychological thrillers, the kind where the killers were always smart, always methodical, and always a little too close to real life. Her books sold well enough to make her a fixture in the local literary scene but not well enough to catapult her out of it. Reese's infamous takedown of her last novel, The Unraveling, had left her reputation battered. "A derivative mess," he'd written. "Lanes is an author who knows how to build suspense but has no idea how to finish what she starts."

Publicly, Margot had laughed it off, smiling through gritted teeth at book signings and making self-deprecating jokes about her "controversial reviews." But behind closed doors, her friends said she'd become distant, her sunny disposition replaced by long silences and dark mutterings about how Reese didn't understand her work—and didn't want to.

When Reese was found dead, his vomit staining the pages of his latest book, Margot was an obvious suspect. The police found traces of a heated email exchange between the two, one where Margot had allegedly called Reese "a parasite who feeds on the brilliance of others." And then there was Margot's description of a cafe and method of killing with eerie similarity in one of her earlier novels.

But if Margot was guilty, she wasn't letting it show. She maintained her innocence with the calm demeanor of someone used to weaving fiction. Yet, in the way her lips tightened when the police questioned her, or how her hands lingered too long on her coffee cup during interviews, there was something off. Something that made even the most sympathetic believe she might just be capable of turning her next bestseller into a true story.

Reynolds took a seat, maintaining eye contact. "Ms. Lanes I want to talk to you about book reviewer Calvin Reese and your relationship with him."

Lanes' expression shifted, the warmth of the café fading. "Why? What happened?"

"Mr. Reese collapsed and died yesterday," the Detective said, gauging Lane's reaction. "We believe it may be murder." The words hung in the air, and for a long moment, neither woman said anything.

A shadow passed over Lane's face, and for a moment, she seemed lost in thought. "I didn't know him that well, but I know firsthand that his reviews can be... devastating."

"You received a harsh review from him recently didn't you?" Reynolds pressed, her tone polite but firm. "How did that affect you?"

Lanes's voice trembled slightly. "Well I'll be honest… it was brutal. I poured my heart into that book, and he tore it apart and for no other reason than to try to make himself look good and to sell newspapers. I was devastated," she explained.

Reynolds leaned in, her curiosity piqued. "Did you ever feel angry enough to confront him about it?"

"To be honest I had thought about it," Lanes admitted, her gaze dropping to her hands. "But it was more frustration than anything else. I wouldn't harm him. I wanted to prove him wrong, not kill him. But he was such a smug ass that I sure can see how someone might want to off him," she said.

"But, you two did have a public feud," Reynolds noted. "Have you seen him recently? Any meetings or conversations that stood out?"

"No," Lanes said, shaking her head, her voice growing steadier. "After his review, and that was about 6-7 months ago, I distanced myself. But I did hear about him dying at the café yesterday. Do they know how? It was such a shock…"

"Did you ever meet Author Ethan Cole?" The Detective asked, watching for any flicker of recognition.

"Ethan? No. I've heard of him, of course. I know they had issues," she replied, her brow furrowing. "I didn't think it was that serious, though."

"Serious enough for someone to want him dead," Reynolds muttered, more to herself than to Lanes. The young Detective had come to understand that the tension in the literary community could ignite a firestorm of emotions.

"What are you saying?" Lanes's voice raised slightly, panic creeping in.

"I'm saying that if there's any connection between you, Ethan Cole, and Calvin Reese, we need to know and we need to know now. Someone wanted Reese dead, and I want and need to make sure you're not involved," Reynolds said.

Lanes's eyes widened, her breaths coming in rapid succession. "I swear, I didn't do anything! I just write about…" her voice trailing off.

Reynolds held up a hand, calming her. "Ms. Lanes I'm not accusing you, but we need to understand the landscape here. Writers can be fiercely protective of their work, and rejection can lead to unexpected consequences. Anyone else who may have felt similarly hurt by Reese's reviews? Who else would want him dead?"

Lanes's lips pursed in thought, and after a long pause, she said, "There was one other author… a Jillian Hargrove. She was furious about his latest review 2-3 months ago. I think you should talk to her," she said.

"Where can I find her?" Reynolds asked, scribbling.

"She's hosting a book signing at the library today in fact," Lanes replied, her expression suddenly anxious. "Just… please, keep my name out of it."
Reynolds nodded, sensing the weight of Lane's fear.

"Will do. I'll get to the bottom of this eventually. Just keep your phone on you in case we need to reach you," she said.

As Reynolds stood to leave, Lane's voice stopped her. "Detective… do you think it was really murder?" she asked. Reynolds paused, her mind heavy with uncertainty. "I think someone wanted him silenced, and we need to find out who that was before it's too late. It's not a natural death."

The chill in the autumn air seemed to deepen as Reynolds stepped back into the bustling city, the noise of life swirling around her. The investigation was unfurling quickly like a dark tapestry in the wind with each breeze leading her closer to the heart of the matter. She was in a a place where ambition could twist into something more deadly. With a new name on her list, she felt a renewed sense of purpose. Author Jillian Hargrove might just hold the key to uncovering the truth, and Detective Reynolds was determined to find out how deep the rancor ran in this world of words.

CHAPTER 8

Questions and Answers… oh My!
The Case against Cole Thickens

A week had passed and when the day was done and evening began its march, Detective Ava Reynolds arrived back at the 10th precinct. She and Mills had spent the entire day questioning witnesses from the Cafe and Reeses' funeral.

Back at the station house Detective Ana Reynolds' mind buzzed with Lila March's chilling parting words at the funeral as she stared at the cork board in her office. On it was the victim in the center and all the major suspects around it like spoke in a wheel. First among equals was Author Ethan Cole with Michael Hawthorne a close second. She knew her next move couldn't wait. She opened her laptop and began combing through everything she had on Calvin Reese. If there was a network of people who operated like him—blackmailers, manipulators, career destroyers—they'd left traces.

The hours slipped by as she sifted through Reese's emails, financials, and social media activity. Reese had been meticulous, but he wasn't invincible. Reynolds' patience paid off when she found something tucked away in his financial records: recurring payments to a company called Argent Associates. It was more than meets the eye.

The company was a dead-end on paper—a vague consulting firm with no discernible services or employees. But Reynolds noticed the payments coincided with key moments in Reese's career: when he published his most damning reviews, when rival critics suddenly vanished from the scene, and when publishing scandals broke.

Argent Associates wasn't just a consulting firm; it was Reese's shield and sword.

Reynolds didn't wait. She reached out to her best analyst a Financial Forensic Specialist Officer Jacob Morris, a tech-savvy investigator with a knack for cracking code, spreadsheets and hidden connections.

"You've got something here," Morris said, walking into her office with a laptop under his arm.

"Yeah," Reynolds said, pointing to the payment records. "Argent Associates. We need to find out who they really are."

Morris nodded and got to work, his fingers flying over the keyboard. Minutes turned into hours as Reynolds paced behind him.

Finally, Morris leaned back, a grim smile on his face. "Argent Associates is a front. The actual organization is called The Coterie."

Reynolds frowned. "The Coterie?"

"It's a small group of elite industry insiders—critics, publishers, editors—it appears to be a consortium that exchanges favors, secrets, and influence. They prop up their own careers while sabotaging anyone who gets in their way," Morris explained. "And Reese wasn't just a member; he was their attack dog. A literary assassin!"

Reynolds' stomach sank. If what Morris was saying was true, Lila's claims weren't just paranoia. She'd taken on a shadowy network of powerful people, and Calvin Reese's murder was only the first shoe to drop and this group is virtually unknown.

"Who's running it?" Reynolds asked.

Morris shook his head. "That's the hard part. They're careful. Everything goes through layers of shell companies and proxies. But…" he hesitated.

"But what?" she said.

"I found a name buried in an old email thread Reese had archived," Jacob said. "It was about a problem with someone named 'Cole'. It's not much, but it's a start. Any idea who that is?"

The name 'Cole' was both a clue and a taunt. Reynolds leaned back in her chair, "I know who that is! That's Author Ethan Cole. He and Reese have been fighting each other for years," she said. "We're welllllll aware of him."

Reynolds and Mills continued the questioning of Reese's 'known associates': Next up is Margaret Kane, a senior editor at Loomis Publishing. Kane had attended Reese's funeral, but didn't sign the guest book and her name hadn't stood out until now. Margaret Kane's office was every bit as imposing as her reputation. The walls were lined with awards, and pictures of her with various celebrities and government leaders. Her desk was a fortress of manuscripts and leather-bound notebooks.

"Detective Reynolds," Margaret said, rising from her chair and offering a practiced smile. "Welcome! To what do I owe this pleasure?"

She didn't waste any time, Reynolds liked that. "I'm investigating the murder of Calvin Reese. You were very close with him, yes?" she asked.

Kane's smile faltered, but she recovered quickly. "Calvin was a colleague, nothing more."

"You attended his funeral?" she asked.

"It's what one does in our world," Kane said coolly.

Reynolds placed a folder on her desk. Inside were copies of Reese's financial records, including the payments to Argent Associates.

"Tell me about 'The Coterie'," Reynolds said, watching Lane's reaction carefully.

The editor's face didn't move, but the Detective noticed her hands tighten on her glass.

"The what? I have no idea what you're talking about," Lane said, her voice steady and defensive.
"Really? Because your name comes up not once but several times in connection with Calvin's financial dealings and that group. You two weren't just

colleagues—you were partners... correct?" she asked watching for any deception.

Lane leaned back, her mask of calm cracking slightly. "Detective, I'd be very careful with your accusations there. You're playing in a world you don't understand."

Reynolds didn't flinch. "Try me."

Lane studied her, then sighed. "Calvin had his enemies, yes. He also had his allies. We look out for each other. That's all. Its no big secret."

"Do you know anyone who wanted him dead? Ever heard the names Cole or Hawthorn?" she asked.

The question hit its mark. Lane's eyes flickered with recognition, though she quickly tried to hide it.

"I don't know anyone by that name," she said.

Reynolds leaned forward, lowering her voice. "Margaret, I'm just after Reese's killer... You can either help me, or you can go down with the ship."

Lane hesitated, the weight of the threat hanging between them. Finally, she spoke.

"I have heard both of those names," she admitted. "Those two authors in particular hated my Calvin. They hang out at a private club called 'The Writer's

Den'... my Calvin was a member and I think so are Cole and Hawthorn," she said.

"Thanks very much, I'll be in touch," said Reynolds as she headed out the door. She wanted to see the club first hand but had a few stops to make first.

Detective Ana Reynolds leaned back in her chair, the pieces of the puzzle scattering across her mind like shards of broken glass. Lila March was a zealot, but she wasn't the poisoner. The Coterie was a sinister network, but their orchestration wasn't meticulous enough for this kill. Calvin Reese's murder felt personal, surgical in its execution. And the name that kept circling back, like a whisper in the storm, was Ethan Cole. Hawthorn was written off because he was in the bag most of the time and was headed for a 28 day program in Arizona.

Cole, the celebrated author whose latest book Reese had savaged just weeks before his death. Cole, who had been at the funeral in disguise, lurking like a shadow. And now, Cole, who had come to the investigation's attention. The outright hatred the two had was well known, so much so that it almost ruled Cole out as a suspect... almost.

Reynolds and Mills knew it was past time for a visit. Ethan Cole lived in brownstone walk-up on the city's west side. When Reynolds arrived she rang the bell and after a moment, the door creaked open. Cole stood there, dressed casually in jeans and a sweater, his face lined with fatigue. But his eyes—sharp and calculating—gave nothing away.

"I'll bet you're Detective Reynolds," he said, his tone calm. "I wasn't expecting company just yet."

"Have we met before?" she asked, stepping inside without waiting for an invitation.

Cole closed the door behind her, his movements unhurried. "No but I assume this is about Calvin Reese so... I knew you would get to me eventually"

"Smart guess." Reynolds turned to face him, her eyes locked onto his. "You were at his funeral?"

He smiled faintly, as though amused. "Guilty. I wanted to see who else would show up."

"Not many people disguise themselves for that kind of curiosity," Reynolds said. "Or poison their critics."

Cole's smile vanished. "Poison? You think I killed him?"

"I don't think, Ethan. I know," she said.

Cole sat down at the small kitchen table, his hands folded in front of him. "You're making a mistake, Detective. Calvin Reese was a parasite, yes, but I didn't kill him."

Reynolds leaned against the counter, crossing her arms. "You're lying. You hated him. You had a motive: he tore your book apart, damaged your career. And you were at the Cafe the day he died."

Cole's face remained impassive, but Reynolds saw the tension in his jaw. "Prove it!" he said defiantly.

"We'll do exactly that sir," she shot back.

After a few moments of silence…"Do you know what it's like, Detective?" he asked softly. "To pour your soul into something, only for someone like Reese to rip it apart just for sport? To see your work reduced to a punchline, your reputation dragged through the mud?"

"That doesn't justify murder," Reynolds said.

"No," he agreed. "But it explains it, doesn't it?"

Reynolds stepped closer. "You slipped the poison into his coffee. You waited until he was distracted— maybe talking to the barista, or checking his phone. Then you walked away, knowing no one would suspect you!"

Cole chuckled darkly. "I love it when you try to do comedy! You've got it all figured out, don't you?"

"Enough to put you away," she asserted.

"Take your best shot!" Cole said being cocky.

After another 10 minutes of good cop, bad cop Cole's demeanor shifted, the mask of calm slipping. He ran a hand through his hair, his voice rising.

"Fine! Yes, I hated him!" he said. "He deserved to suffer for what he did to me and to countless others. But I didn't kill him."

"Then who did?" she pressed.

Cole hesitated, his eyes flickering toward the window. The rain outside seemed to press against the glass in a suffocating way.

"I don't know, take your pick" he said finally. "But whoever it was… they had more reason than I did. Reese wasn't just a critic, Detective. He was a predator. He ruined lives for fun, for sport and he didn't care about the consequences."

Reynolds studied him, her instincts warring with her logic. Cole's anger was genuine, his words raw. But was he telling the truth?

"Do you expect me to believe you're innocent?" she asked incredulously.

Cole stood, his hands clenched into fists. "Believe whatever you want. But ask yourself this: if I killed him, why would I stick around? Why go to his funeral? Why not just disappear?"

Reynolds didn't answer. And after a few moments of her studying his face and without saying another word she walked out the door. As she drove away from his house, she couldn't shake the feeling that the case wasn't as clear-cut as everyone hoped. Cole had motive and opportunity, but his defense and explanation felt...honest and sincere.

Back at the precinct, Reynolds reviewed the evidence again. Lila March, The Coterie, Ethan Cole —every thread that led to or from Critic Calvin Reese, but none of them tied together neatly. The toxicology report which was due shortly would help to clarify things.

Then she saw it: a detail she'd overlooked before. The barista at the Cafe, the one who'd taken Calvin's order, had been fired the day after the murder. Reynolds hadn't thought much of it at the time, but now the timing felt odd and suspicious.

She picked up her phone and called. "Get me everything you can on the Cafe staff," she said. "Especially the barista who served Calvin Reese."

Officer Miller's reply was quick. "On it."

As Reynolds hung up, a chill ran down her spine. The pieces were shifting again, and the picture they formed was darker than she'd imagined. It was clear that this was murder with many suspects.

Later that evening the Detective and her partner hit the club Lane had told them about. A high-end, members-only club called 'The Writer's Den' that had members from across the publishing and media world. It was a known haunt for the elite—a place where deals were made, alliances were formed, and secrets were whispered. Average drink price? $20!

Detective Reynolds and her partner Officer Mills entered under the guise of a husband and wife writing team looking to network. The club was dimly lit, its walls lined with bookshelves and portraits of literary icons. Groups of people huddled over cocktails, their conversations too quiet to overhear. It was almost like something out of the 1940s. Old school and monied.

They split up to work the room for intel. Reynolds made her way to the bar, scanning the room. She was looking for someone—anyone—who might lead her in the direction of the killer. A man approached her, his tailored suit impeccable.

"You look lost," he said, his smile warm and his delivery more than smooth.

"Just tryin to find the right people to talk to," Reynolds replied, keeping her voice casual.

The man smirked. "In a place like this, the right people find you!"

Before Reynolds could respond, her phone buzzed in her pocket. She glanced at the screen and froze. It was a text message, sent from an unknown number:

"You're getting warmer, Detective."

Her pulse quickened as she looked up. The man in the suit had vanished...absorbed into the party.

Her hand tightened around her phone as she stared at the cryptic message. The words were unsettling, yet they confirmed one thing: she was being watched and she was rattling the right cages.

She glanced around the dimly lit club, trying to mask her unease. The opulent surroundings—the leather armchairs, the soft murmur of conversation, and the clink of crystal glasses—felt like a gilded trap. If 'The Coterie' operated here, she needed to tread lightly. They were like the mafia.

Reynolds flagged down a server carrying a tray of martinis. "Excuse me," she said, slipping into the role of an ambitious writer. "I'm a new writer here and I'm looking to make some connections. Who would you recommend I talk to?"

The server studied her for a moment, then gestured toward a corner booth. "That's Eleanor Grayson. She runs a major PR firm for top-tier authors. But, uh, be careful—she only talks to people worth her time and no offense, I don't think that's you!"

Reynolds followed the server's gaze to a striking woman in her late fifties, impeccably dressed in a blue pantsuit with white pearls, sipping a glass of $100 a bottle red wine. Her sharp eyes scanning the room, calculatingly and cool.

Reynolds approached with confidence, carrying a drink she didn't intend to sip. Grayson glanced up as the Detective reached her table with an expression that was both neutral but expectant.

"Ms. Eleanor Grayson?" Reynolds asked.

"Yes," Grayson replied, her voice clipped.

"I'm Ana. I've heard about your work and was hoping for a few minutes of your time. I'm working on a piece about power dynamics in the literary world. Do you have a moment?"

Grayson arched an eyebrow. "Power dynamics? That's a delicate topic."

"I find that the most interesting stories are," Reynolds said smoothly, sliding into the booth across from her.

Eleanor's lips curved into a faint smile. "Interesting approach. You must be new. What's your angle?"

Reynolds chose her words carefully. "I want to understand how influence is wielded behind the scenes—how reputations are built or destroyed.

Calvin Reese, the reviewer who just died, his name came up during my research."

The mention of Reese caused a flicker of something in Grayson's eyes—annoyance or concern, Reynolds couldn't tell.

"Calvin was... provocative," Grayson said, her tone measured. "But he played the game well. Too well, perhaps."

Reynolds leaned forward slightly. "And what about The Coterie? Was that part of the game?"

Grayson's expression turned icy. "I don't know what you're talking about."

"Don't you?" She pressed, keeping her voice steady. "Because from what I've gathered, Calvin wasn't acting alone. There's a network protecting people like him—propping up some, burying others. And I think you know more than you're letting on."

Grayson's fingers tightened around her wineglass. For a moment, Ana thought she might walk away. But instead, Eleanor leaned in, her voice a sharp whisper. "You're poking around in places you don't belong, Ms. Reynolds. My advice? Drop it. Before you find yourself in over your head."

Reynolds held her gaze. "Is that a warning or a threat?"

Eleanor smirked and took a sip of her wine. "It's a reality check. Calvin Reese had tons of enemies take your pick. But I think you are off to a good start with those two!"

The conversation with Grayson confirmed Reynolds' suspicions—The Coterie wasn't just real; it was dangerous. But she needed more.

As she moved to the bar, her phone buzzed again. Another unknown number, another message:

"Still chasing shadows, Detective? Try the hors d'oeuvres!"

Reynolds's heart raced as she glanced toward the club's glass doors leading to a outdoor terrace where the hors d'oeuvres and cash bar were set up. Whoever was sending these messages was watching.

She stepped outside, the cool night air a welcome reprieve from the club's stifling atmosphere. The terrace was nearly empty, save for some couples and a man leaning against the railing, a cigarette glowing in his hand.

He turned as Reynolds approached, his face partially shadowed. Late thirties, slicked-back hair, Rolex and a tailored suit that screamed wealth.

"You're persistent," he said, his voice low and smooth. "I'll give you that."

"And you are?" she asked, masking her uneasiness.

"Someone who values discretion," he replied, exhaling a stream of smoke. "Let's just say I've been… Calvin's nemesis for a while now."

"What do you know about 'The Coterie'?"

The man chuckled. "Jumping straight to the heart of it, huh? Bold. I respect that."

"Please answer my question," Reynolds said, her tone firm and polite.

He took another drag of his cigarette. "The Coterie isn't just a group, Detective. It's an idea. A shared understanding among people who know how to survive in this business. Power isn't given; it's taken. Calvin understood that. Maybe too well."

"Who are you?" Reynolds asked.

The man's demeanor shifted, his easy confidence hardening. "Now you're asking dangerous questions."

"Dangerous for who?" she asked.

"For anyone who doesn't know when to stop," he responded. The man crushed his cigarette and stepped closer, his voice dropping to a whisper.

"Walk away, Detective. This isn't your world. And if you keep digging, I fear it won't end well for you." He turned and disappeared into the crowed club, leaving her alone on the terrace.

Back in her car, Reynolds replayed the encounters in her mind and wrote in her documentation notebook. Grayson's veiled threats, the cryptic man on the terrace, the text messages—it all pointed to one thing: she was closer to finding the killer than she realized, and they knew it.

Her phone buzzed with a text one last time.

"You're out of your depth, Detective. Let this go before you drown. There are sharks here!"

She stared at the message, her jaw tightening. She was out of her depth? Perhaps but like a Pit Bull with a bone, she wasn't about to let it go.

The weight of the day was still heavy on her shoulders. The revelations from her meeting with Author Margot Lanes had set off alarm bells in her mind, and she knew the investigation needed to move more quickly. But nothing could prepare her for the next turn of events.

"Detective Reynolds!" Officer Mills called out as she entered, his voice cutting through the buzz of activity in the precinct. He was at his desk, his eyes wide with urgency. "You really need to see this!"

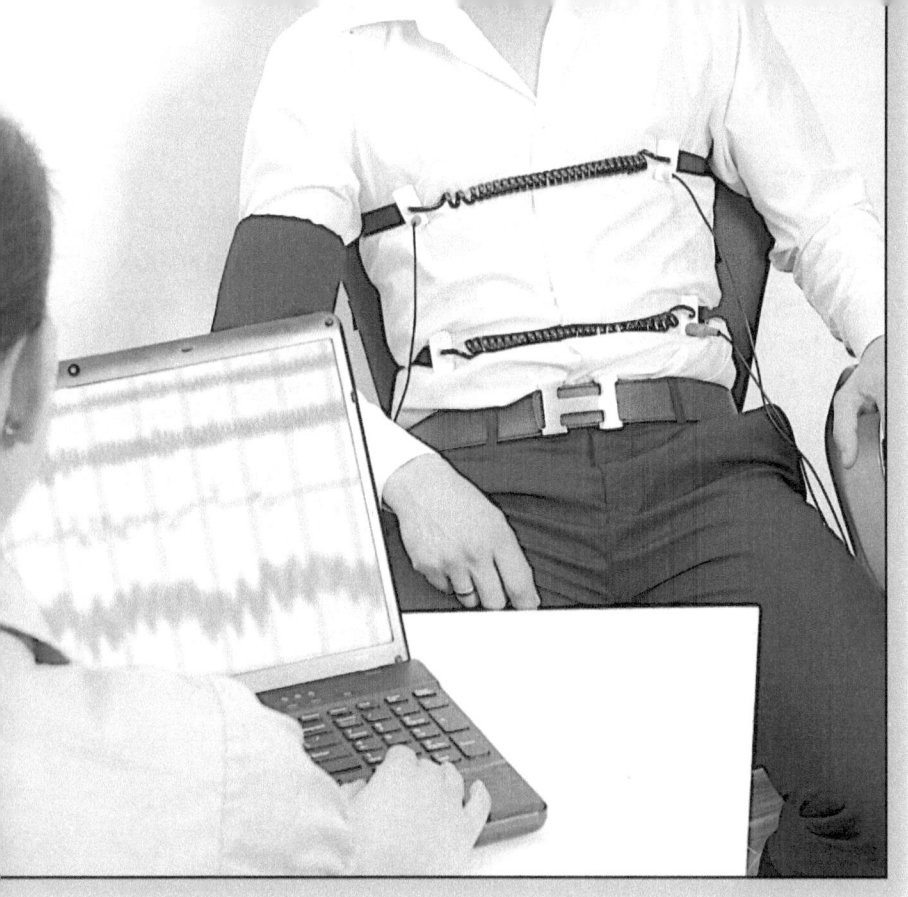

"What is it?" she asked impatiently, her pulse quickening.

Mills handed her a stack of papers, his expression grave. "Ethan Cole was just brought in for questioning! The DA wants him charged with the murder of media reviewer Calvin Reese."

Reynolds felt the ground shift beneath her. "What?! How the hell did this happen? You'd think that the damn DA would at least touch base with the investigating team and the lead Detective!" she said incredulously. "They really need to coordinate better. If they blow this I'm really gonna be pissed!"

Mills explained, "After you left the cafe, we got a tip from the barista that she recognized Cole's face from the security camera footage. She confirmed he was there near the time of the incident, and he was seen leaving just moments after Reese collapsed," he said. "We pulled his credit card transactions, and he bought two copies of 'Death Pages' the day before at a small little known bookstore across town. The timing is just too coincidental, isn't it?" Mills asked.

"Damn it," she muttered, shaking her head. "We need to be careful here. I spoke with him just hours ago, and he seemed genuinely shaken by Reese's death. We can't jump to conclusions. We need to get our shit together and make these charges stick."

"I know," Mills said, his voice steady. "The evidence is mounting against him. Things are moving fast! About 45 minutes ago we found some poisons in Cole's office. The forensic team has the ball and is still analyzing it all, but we have enough to hold him for sure."

"Where is he now?" Reynolds asked, her mind racing. She was usually 3 steps ahead of other cops.

"He's in holding. The Captain via the DA wants you to question him and I can take you to him if ya want," Mills said.

"Ummmm I know the way," she said her gut churning. She needed to see Cole for herself anyway, to gauge his reaction now that the noose was tightening around him. She followed Mills through the labyrinthine of halls of the precinct until they reached the small 15x20' interrogation room. The one with puke-green walls.

Inside, award-winning author Ethan Cole sat at a small metal table, his once-rugged and handsome looks now drawn and pale. The shadows beneath his eyes told a story of sleepless nights and overwhelming stress. When he saw Reynolds, his expression shifted from anger to confusion.

"Detective," Cole said, his voice hoarse. "I didn't do this. Please you have to believe me!"

She took a seat across from him, looking directly into his eyes. "Sir have you been read your rights?

"Yes I have. My new attorney is on her way," he said. The vibe in the room was starting to mellow.

"May I call you Ethan? Would you like some coffee? I hope you know we're here to help you. I want to get your side of the story. We don't want to jump to conclusions, but you need to be honest with me, OK?" she asked. "Did you kill Calvin Reese?"

He took a long pause. "No. I didn't," he insisted, his voice rising slightly. "I was in the cafe all the time, yes, but I didn't poison him. I had nothing to do with it! And the polygraph will tell you that I'm not lying. If my lawyer says it's ok."

"Then I have two very important questions for you, Ethan..." she said, and the room went silent for a prolonged time. "One, how did you know it was poison that killed him, and two, why was the same poison found in your office!? Reynolds pressed, her tone firm and accusing.

"I want my attorney," he said. Cole sat in silence for awhile and was devastated that someone he thought of as an ally was now accusing him of murder. He had a close working relationship with the police for researching his books.

Breaking the silence Reynolds said, "And Ethan, you were seen leaving the café just after he collapsed. It looks real bad for you, sir!"

"I was working! I didn't really see him until after it happened. I would never... I couldn't! I was upset, sure, but I wouldn't kill someone over a damn review. That's insane!" His hands trembled as he spoke and he made sure desperation was evident in his eyes and voice. He has rehearsed this in the mirror many times becoming the consummate actor weaving the fiction of his innocence.

Reynolds studied him, weighing his words. She had felt the authenticity in his distress during their earlier conversation, but the mounting evidence made it difficult to overlook. "Then please help me understand. If you didn't do it, who did? Who else had reason to want him dead?" While Reynolds questioned Cole Sergeant Mills sat across the room studying him closely.

"How should I know? I don't know! He had a lot of enemies," Cole replied, frustration seeping into his voice. "He was a jerk and a ruthless critic. He had no qualms about destroying someone's career over minutia. Someone needs to look into that! Look at Margot Lanes—she was furious over his last review. She might have had a motive!" he said.

"Lanes is a possible lead, yes, but you need to understand something sir," Reynolds said, her voice steady but urgent. "You're the one in custody right now. You have been charged. You're the prime suspect. If you can provide any evidence that supports your innocence, now would be a damn good time to do it. A rare poison has been found in your office sir! If you have any explanation, anything at all, we'd love to hear it," she said.

Cole ran a hand through his disheveled hair, a flicker of panic crossing his face. "It's a plant! I swear I didn't do this! I was just trying to get my life back together after his review! I wanted to prove him wrong, not kill him." He was an extremely convincing liar with well rehearsed responses.

The door to the interrogation room swung open, and Mills stepped in, his expression serious. "Detective, the forensic team also found something else in Ethan's office that's quite interesting."

"What now?" Reynolds asked, knowing the answer.

"A notebook with drafts of his new novel, but it also includes journal entries. It seems he was fixated on Reese, detailing their interactions and his thoughts about the reviews. There are some pretty dark passages in there, talking about how he wished Reese would just disappear."

Cole's expression hardened at this news, and he glared at Mills. "That was just my frustration. That doesn't mean I wanted him dead! Anyone who writes can tell you that, you idiot. It's called artistic expression!" he said.

Reynolds turned to Mills, "How dark are we talking here? I mean is it a confession?"

"There are passages with things like 'If only critics could taste their own poison' and 'What if words had consequences?'" Mills replied, his voice low.

"Ethan, you need to understand the implications of this," Reynolds said, her tone growing even more serious. "It's not just words on a page now; it's a narrative that can be interpreted in many ways…all of them bad for you. Right now, it looks very much like you had a motive and the means to kill him."

"I didn't mean it literally!" he shouted, slamming his palms on the table. "This is all a nightmare! You have to find the real killer! Somebody put that poison in my office. I don't want to be framed for this!" Cole said obviously beside himself.

Reynolds leaned closer, her eyes searching him for sincerity. "Then help me Ethan. If you can prove you were set up, if you have anyone you can think of who might have had access to that book, please let me know," she said. "Otherwise? You are going to the Gas Chamber!"

Ethan looked down at the table, his fingers trembling. "I… I was working with a woman on a book cover design. Her name is Rachel. She's from South America and knows me and my work. Maybe she saw something?" Cole was fabricating a narration that would work and was willing cast aspirations on any and all.

"Rachel who?" Mills asked, jotting down notes.

"Rachel Sanchez. She's a graphic designer. I had her work on the cover for my new book 'Death from Within'," Ethan replied, desperation creeping into his voice. "Maybe she knows about the chemicals and poison? If she can vouch for my whereabouts… or if she knows anything about Reese, she might help," Cole said as he grasped at straws while weaving the lie even further and trying to cast suspicion in any other direction.

Reynolds nodded, committing the name to memory. "I'll reach out to her. But you have to stay calm. There's still a chance to clear your name, but you need to cooperate with us… fully. And if I find you have lied to me…" she said as her voice trailed off but the pending doom quite clear.

"I will. I swear I'll do anything to prove my innocence!" said the Author.

"Including lying your ass off," Mills thought to himself. As he stood up to leave, Reynolds gave him a look that said what they both now knew… that there was a 90% probability that Author Ethan Cole was the killer. She took a moment to gather her thoughts. The weight of the investigation was pressing heavily upon her, the intricate web of ambition and betrayal tightening with each passing moment. She needed to move quickly if she was to unravel the truth before it was too late. But the guilt of him was becoming irrefutable.

"Ethan," she said softly, her voice steady and sympathetic. "We'll get to the bottom of this. But right now, you need to stay focused. Stay calm. Let's see if Rachel can provide the answers we need."

With that, she left the interrogation room, the door closing with a finality that echoed to all present. As she headed back to her cubical, the pieces of the puzzle began to form a clearer picture, and the more she thought about it, the larger the shadows of doubt loomed as to who truly held the pen in this deadly tale. The clock was ticking, and she had to find Rachel before the lie of Cole's poison story spread further, ensnaring someone else in its path. For

Reynolds, part of her was disappointed as she had hoped Cole was innocent.

No matter how charming he was and he was very, Detective Ana Reynolds didn't buy Ethan Cole's innocence. No matter how eloquently he defended himself, guilt seeped from his every word, a subtle tremor in his voice when Calvin Reese's name came up. His rage at Reese was palpable—righteous, even. But the Detective and her partner had seen it too many times before: righteous anger often turned to deadly rage and resolve to kill.

After she and Mills conferred back at the station they decided to push Cole harder.

The next morning, the two returned to Ethan Cole's, this time with a warrant. They didn't bother knocking. Cole's face was a mix of alarm, annoyance and resignation as he saw Reynolds and two uniformed officers walk thru the door.

"You really don't let things go, do you?" Cole said, stepping aside to let them in. "Ever hear of knocking? You got a warrant pretty officer?"

"Yes I do," Reynolds said flatly, pulling on a pair of gloves as she walked past. "You've got secrets, Mr. Cole. Let's just see where you're hiding them!"

As the officers began searching the home, Cole leaned against the kitchen doorway, arms crossed.

"Do you think this'll change anything? You're looking for a smoking gun that doesn't exist."

"We'll just see about that!" said Mills.

Reynolds made her way to Cole's home office, where a large desk sat covered in neatly arranged papers, a computer, and a stack of books. The shelves around the room were lined with literary works, many of them Cole's own novels. The walls were filled with photos and awards. Across the room was a long table with chemistry equipment, microscope, small refrigerator and a small cage.

"What's this?" Reynolds muttered, picking up a leather-bound journal. The pages were filled with notes, outlines, and drafts. Toward the back, however, the tone shifted. The handwriting became erratic, the words darker.

Reynolds flipped through the journal as Cole watched her from the doorway, his calm demeanor now replaced with unease.

"'He deserved it,'" she read aloud. "'Every word he wrote was poison, every review a dagger. Maybe it's time he tasted his own medicine!'"

Cole's jaw tightened. "It's just writing. A healthy way to vent negative thoughts."

Mills raised an eyebrow. "A way to rehearse, you mean?"

"You're really reaching," Cole snapped.

Reynolds continued reading: "'Reese thinks he's untouchable, but he's not. One well-placed dose—something tasteless, odorless—and he's gone. Justice served. Completely untraceable. He'll never know, no one will. Ever!'"

The words sent a chill through her. "Sounds more like planning than venting."

"It's just fiction," Cole insisted. "I'm a writer. I explore ideas. That's all this is."

Reynolds stepped closer, the journal still in her hand. "Did you 'explore' these ideas at the Cafe? Was it your fiction that killed Calvin Reese?" she asked.

For the first time, Cole's mask cracked. His calm façade slipped, replaced by a flash of anger.

"Damn it you just don't understand," he said, his voice low. "He wasn't just a critic. He was a butcher. He destroyed people for fun. He ruined me, and he enjoyed it. Do you know what that feels like?"

"I know what murder feels like," Reynolds shot back. "It feels like doom. Like a heavy weight that never leaves you… like you're feeling right now."

One of the officers called out from the living room. "Detective, you might want to see this." Reynolds followed the voice, leaving Cole standing in the office. On the coffee table was a small vial, tucked away in a drawer alongside eye droppers and lab equipment.

"What is it?" She asked, crouching to examine it.

Reynolds's stomach turned. Tasteless, odorless, and precisely the kind of a deadly toxin substance Cole had described in his journal.

She turned to Cole, who had followed her into the room. His face had gone pale, his hands trembling.

"I didn't use it," he said quickly. "I thought about it, but I didn't go through with it. It was just research and its 110% legal"

"Then why do you have it?" Reynolds demanded.
"For protection," Cole said, his voice desperate. "Calvin had enemies. Real enemies. I was afraid someone might come after me, too."

The Detective crossed her arms. "So you bought a lethal poison? That's your story?"

Cole opened his mouth to respond but said nothing. The evidence was enough for them to make an arrest. As the officers handcuffed Cole, he didn't resist. Instead, he looked at Reynolds, his eyes filled with a mix of anger and despair.

"You're wrong," he said. "I didn't kill him. But whomever did... they're not finished. I bet Calvin wasn't the only one on their list!"

The officers didn't respond and they watched as Cole was led out and into the waiting patrol car.

Back at the precinct, Reynolds sat at her desk in here more than tiny office, staring at the journal and the vial of poison. The case against Ethan Cole was strong—motive, opportunity, and damning evidence. But something about his final words gnawed at her. "They're not finished," Reynolds said.

Could Cole be telling the truth? Could there be more to Calvin Reese's death than a single man's vendetta? Reynolds glanced at the cork board behind her desk, where photos of Reese, Lila March, The Coterie, and now Ethan Cole stared back at her. The web of connections was tangled, and far from complete. One thing was certain: it wasn't over.

CHAPTER 9

Busted!
Author Ethan Cole Arrested

T he days following Ethan Cole's arrest dragged on like molasses, thick with tension and uncertainty. The precinct buzzed with the latest gossip about the high-profile murder case, and for veteran Detective Ava Reynolds, the noise only intensified the pressure weighing on her shoulders. With the trial looming, the stakes had never been higher for Ethan—or for her own integrity and rep as a detective.

In the dim light of her precinct cubical, she scanned through the mountains of paperwork stacked haphazardly on her desk. Witness statements, forensic reports, photos and legal documents lay strewn across the surface, remnants of a frantic search for truth amidst the chaos. The clock ticked loudly in the silence, a constant reminder of the impending trial date and the urgency to uncover evidence that might save Ethan from death or a life behind bars.

"The DA is an idiot! His ambition is gonna let a killer walk. We brought this case way too early," she said to herself.

Cole was already out on bail even though the weight of the charges hanging over him were like a dark rain cloud. Reynolds had seen him a few times since their last conversation, and each encounter revealed the toll the situation was taking on him. The fire that had once burned brightly in his eyes was now replaced with a haunting weariness, the spark of creativity extinguished by fear and desperation.

As she flipped through a notebook filled with her observations, a knock on her door interrupted her thoughts. It was Mills, his expression serious as he stepped inside.

"Hey, Detective," he said, taking a seat across from her. "I just got off the phone with Cole's lawyer. They're building a defense strategy, and they want to meet with us."

Reynolds raised an eyebrow. "His lawyer? I work for the state not the defense besides I thought he was going with the public defender?"

"Looks like he managed to secure a better option. A big-name attorney, Veronica Pierce, has taken him on as a client. She has a reputation for getting clients off against overwhelming odds," Mills explained.

"Great. Just what we need—more theatrics in a case that's already spiraled out of control," Reynolds said, running a hand through her hair. "Is the DA Ok with us talking to them?"

"He said its a two way street. She's known for her sharp instincts and persuasive arguments," Mills replied. "The DA said maybe we can pick up what their strategy might be and pass it on to him."

"Let's see what she has to say, then." Reynolds' voice was firm as she closed her notebook. "If we can gather any evidence that points to his guilt, it'll strengthen our case against him."

They made their way to the meeting room, where Cole was already waiting. He sat at the table, looking more put together than during their last encounter, but the tension was evident in the way he gripped the edge of the table. His lawyer had yet to arrive and he looked a little lonely sitting there.

"Mr. Cole," Reynolds greeted him, her expression serious. "I hope you've had some time to think seriously about your situation."

"I have," Ethan replied, his voice steadier. "I know I'm innocent, but I'm worried about what they're saying. I need you both to help me find the truth." He was serious about maintaining a facade of innocence.

"That's up to your Lawyer and your team now," Reynolds said.

Ethan Cole had always been a man who lived in the gray areas of life—morally, legally, and especially when it came to the women who drifted in and out of his orbit. Attraction, for Ethan, was less about connection and more about power. He didn't just notice women; he studied them, dissecting their movements, their words, and the way their laughter shifted depending on who they were trying to impress. He collected their attention like trophies, each one feeding a need he couldn't quite satisfy.

From the moment Attorney Veronica Pierce walked into the room, Ethan was hooked. He had contracted her earlier but she was out of the country. She was everything he admired and everything he feared: commanding, sharp, and utterly uninterested in his charm. When she leaned across the table in her crimson blazer, her piercing green eyes locking with his as she outlined his defense strategy, Ethan felt a familiar itch—a pull he recognized as both desire and danger. She wasn't not like the others; Veronica didn't swoon, didn't simper. She matched his arrogance with her own, and that made him want her even more.

But Cole's attraction wasn't exclusive, nor was it ever simple. He had a way of seeing potential in every woman he met—a muse, a conquest, or sometimes both. There was Margot Lanes, the author he'd once mentored and toyed with emotionally, her adoration turning bitter when he dismissed her work as mediocre. There was the young bookstore clerk who blushed every time he signed a copy of his latest novel, a fleeting obsession that barely lasted the length of a tour. Even his relationship with his late wife was fleeting, her disappearance had thrust him into the headlines long before Calvin Reese's murder. She had once been the center of his universe—until she wasn't.

For Cole, women were characters in his own story, tools to be wielded or obstacles to be overcome. And yet, with Veronica, it felt different. She wasn't a character he could write; she was the author of her own script, and that infuriated and excited him in equal measure. Cole wasn't sure if he wanted to win her over or simply see if he could. Either way, it was a game he couldn't resist playing, even as the walls of his life closed in around him. He knew he shouldn't have spoken with the police but his big mouth and gregarious nature made that impossible. She was furious with him and with the local police.

For all his talent at creating villains and victims on the page, Ethan Cole had never learned the art of restraint in the real world. Both with his mouth and his heart. And after some initial flirtations with Veronica Pierce, he wasn't sure if he was seducing her—or if she was simply letting him believe he could do so. Veronica Pierce was the kind of woman who could stop traffic just by stepping onto the sidewalk! Her presence was electric, impossible to ignore, and intentional. She didn't just enter a room; she commanded it, every step in her stilettos echoing like a declaration. The press had a nickname for her: 'The Viper', and she wore it like a badge of honor. She was smart, cunning and beautiful.

She was a tall woman, curvaceous in a way that made people underestimate her intelligence—once.

Her dark hair was a cascade of waves, always perfectly styled, framing a face that could shift from flirtatious charm to icy resolve in a heartbeat. Her red lipstick was her signature, a warning as much as an accessory, and her tailored suits were works of art, sculpted to her like armor and costing a small fortune. Her BMW parked outside was six figures.

Her voice was as striking as the rest of her—low, rich, and laced with razor-sharp wit. Pierce had a gift for dismantling her opponents in the courtroom, her words precise and devastating, like a surgeon wielding a scalpel. Judges respected her, juries feared her, and prosecutors loathed her. She didn't just defend her clients; she made you question why you ever doubted their innocence in the first place.

Representing Cole wasn't just a case for Veronica—it was a spectacle she lived for. The media circus, the whispers of his guilt, the lurid details of the crime—it was the kind of challenge she thrived on. She stood by his side at press conferences, a picture of calculated poise, shutting down reporters with biting quips that left them scrambling for a follow-up. Not only was she easy on the eyes, she was articulate and Pierce was a master at media manipulation. From coming across great on camera defending her clients on TV to having her staff plant positive stories in the media, she was simply the best. For example during the trial she arranged for Cole to visit an after school program for disadvantaged youth to talk about writing and she made sure the local TV News was there when Cole visited a VA Hospital to donate blood.

And Pierce wasn't naive about her client. She'd read all the case files, seen the evidence, and heard the rumors. She knew the odds were not in his favor, but that didn't matter to her. What mattered was winning, and she'd made an art out of turning the odds into her weapon. She was already spinning her narrative: the genius author framed by the jealous and the vengeful, a victim of his own brilliance. Whether she believed it or not was irrelevant.

Her detractors called her ruthless, opportunistic, even soulless, but Veronica didn't care. She thrived on their scorn as much as she did on her victories. And as she prepared to defend Ethan Cole, there was no doubt she'd do whatever it took to win—even if it meant getting her hands a little dirty.

Veronica Pierce entered the room in her $1500 Baruni pantsuit looking as if she was at a fashion show or some sort of spring cotillion. Exuding confidence she took a seat beside the Defendant. Her tailored suit and sharp features commanded attention, and her presence instantly filled the space with an air of authority.

"Detective Reynolds, Officer Mills," she said with a nod, her gaze moving between them. "Thank you for meeting with us. I've reviewed the case files, and it's clear my client is totally innocent. There's more to this than what's being presented by the DA."

Reynolds crossed her arms, intrigued. "There's lots of evidence against Mr. Cole as you well know Ms. Pierce." The two were not hitting it off very well.

"I want to focus on two key aspects," she began, her tone brisk. "First, the timeline. We have established Ethan's whereabouts before and after Calvin Reese's death. We believe we can demonstrate that he was set up," Pierce said. "Second, we have dug into

Calvin Reese's background. He was a controversial figure, and I'm sure there are plenty of people who didn't appreciate his critiques. We don't feel the Police, that's you, have fully explored those connections," Pierce said sarcastically. "You need to cast a wider net," she replied, her eyes sharp. "We'll give you an opportunity to save yourselves some embarrassment and drop the charges so you can find the real killer," Pierce offered. "Lot's of other people had both motive and opportunity," she said.

Ethan's shoulders relaxed slightly, hope flickering in his eyes. "Someone else wanted him dead…"

"Exactly," Pierce said, scribbling notes. "We will speak with Simmons, the graphic designer. If she can vouch for Ethan's whereabouts, that could solidify his defense. I'll reach out to Rachel"

Reynolds said. "We still need to verify your client's story. I want to see if there's a record of his interactions with Reese. I'm also looking into any online interactions—emails, social media," she said. "Reese might have had discussions that could shed light on his relationships," Mills suggested.

With their plan set, the energy in the room shifted. Veronica leaned back in her chair, a smile forming on her lips. "We'll need to move fast. The prosecution, oh wait, you ARE the prosecution! Have you been digging into Ethan's past and trying to paint him as a bitter author with a vendetta?" Pierce asked, already knowing the answer.

166

As they left the meeting room, Reynolds's mind raced with the possibilities. The case had grown murkier, yet the path ahead felt clearer. If they could expose the deeper issues within the literary community and the people surrounding Calvin Reese, they might just uncover the truth before it slipped through their fingers. Then again, Reynolds had came to feel Cole was guilty.

Reynolds felt a fire igniting again within her—a resolve to prosecute Ethan Cole to the fullest extent of the law. She now wanted to expose the intricate web of deceit that Cole had put forth. The trial was fast approaching. The stakes were high, but the pursuit of truth was a battle worth fighting for. If he was guilty he might pay with his life or spend what was left of it in a 6' x 10' cell.

Murderer and author Ethan Cole sat across from Attorney Victoria Pierce in the dimly lit meeting room at the detention center, the faint buzz of fluorescent lights humming above them. She was radiant even in this bleak setting—a tailored navy suit hugging her figure, her hair falling in soft waves around her soft but, no-nonsense face. Her lips, painted a deep red, pursed as she flipped through the latest batch of discovery documents.

"You're making this harder than it has to be, Ethan," she said, her voice low and precise.

He smirked, leaning back in his chair. "That's funny coming from you, Victoria. Isn't it your job to do the impossible?"

Her eyes flicked up to meet his, piercing and unrelenting. "If you want me to defend you, you need to stop playing games and start telling me the truth."

Ethan's smile faded. For a moment, the room seemed to shrink, the space between them charged with something unspoken. "You think you know the truth?" he asked, his voice soft but defiant.

Victoria leaned forward, her hands resting on the table. "I know you're brilliant. I know you're dangerous and cute. And I know you're lying about something. You don't get to charm me like you do everyone else!" she said.

Ethan's gaze locked onto hers, and the air between them thickened. He leaned forward, closing the gap, his voice dropping to a whisper. "What if I'm not lying, Victoria? What if the truth is uglier than you're ready to handle?"

Her breath halted, but she didn't flinch. Instead, her eyes searched his, and for the first time, she saw the vulnerability beneath his carefully constructed arrogance.

"You're a complicated man, Ethan Cole," she murmured, her voice softening.

"And you," he replied, his lips curling into a faint smile, "are simply impossible to ignore."

Before either of them could think better of it, the distance between them vanished. Ethan's hand moved to her cheek, tentative but firm, and their lips met in a kiss that was equal parts heat and desperation. It wasn't soft or tentative—it was a collision of two forces, raw and electric.

Victoria pulled back first, her breath shallow, her eyes wide with shock. "This is a mistake," she said, but her voice betrayed her resolve.

Ethan leaned back, his lips still tingling from the contact. "Maybe," he said, his tone smooth and unapologetic. "But I don't think either of us cares."

Victoria stared at him, her mind racing. She was a professional, and this crossed every line she'd ever drawn for herself. But there was something about Ethan Cole—something magnetic and dangerous—that she couldn't seem to resist. Her hands trembling as she gathered her papers, "We can explore our feelings after the trial and not before."

Ethan gave an alluring smile, leaning back in his chair as if he'd already won. "Understood. But I got one question for ya... who says I need saving, Victoria?" She found him cute when he was flirting.

As she left the room, her heels clicking against the cold tile floor, she realized she didn't care if he was guilty or not, she needed and wanted to save him.

CHAPTER 10

Order in the Court
The State vs Ethan Cole

The courtroom was a mosaic of anxiety and anticipation, the air thick with the scent of polished wood and the quiet murmurs of spectators. The gallery was filled with an eclectic mix of curious onlookers, literary enthusiasts, and journalists eager to witness the drama unfold. The high ceilings loomed above, somehow a stark reminder of the gravity of the proceedings. It was like a scene from the old TV show 'Matlock'. A classic with oak paneling and brass accents!

As Ethan Cole stood at the defendant's table, his heart raced. Today was the day his fate would be decided. Clad in a tailored navy suit that felt more like a shroud than a shield, he faced the judge, the jury, and the reality of the allegations..

"Order, order! Court is now in session," the judge announced, his voice resonating with authority.

The gavel echoed in the silence, and the room settled into a tense quiet. Judge Matthias Sinclair, a man with decades of experience etched into the lines of his face, surveyed his courtroom with a steely gaze. And there was no doubt about whose court room it was.

Cole felt the weight of the judge's scrutiny, his pulse quickening. Next to him, Veronica Pierce flipped through her notes, exuding a calm confidence that contrasted sharply with his inner turmoil. She had assured him that they would navigate this storm together, but as the opening statements commenced, he could feel the doubt creeping into his mind.

The prosecution went first, a sharp-featured DA named David Kline, age 37, who seemed perfectly at ease under the intense spotlight. He adjusted his tie and stepped forward, his presence commanding the jury's attention.

"Ladies and gentlemen of the jury," Kline began, his voice smooth and measured. "You are here to determine whether the defendant, Ethan Cole, is guilty of the murder of Calvin Reese. The evidence we present today will clearly show that Mr. Cole had both motive and opportunity to commit this heinous unprovoked crime."

Ethan's stomach twisted at the words. He had spent sleepless nights reliving the moment Calvin died, grappling with the loss of a man he barely knew but whose words had the power to shatter careers. In his heart Cole felt Reese got exactly what he deserved.

"Mr. Cole was upset, as you'll hear from witnesses. He felt victimized by Reese's reviews, scathing critiques that threatened to unravel his professional life," Kline continued, pacing before the jury with deliberate precision. "But this is not simply a matter of hurt feelings, Calvin Reeses' reviews cost Mr. Cole money and reputation. You will also learn that Mr. Cole went so far as to poison a book—a book titled 'Death Pages' written by the victim. In doing so, he ensured that Reese would not only suffer for his words but would ultimately pay for them with his life. He is guilty of premeditated murder in the first degree. Thank you for your time," he said. The courtroom was dead silent.

The weight of Kline's words landed like a physical blow. Cole's throat tightened as he glanced at the jury, their expressions ranging from skepticism to intrigue. He could feel the tide turning against him even before it had truly begun.

When Kline finally finished, the courtroom felt electric, charged with the momentum of his accusations. The young DA was so good even Cole thought he was guilty! But Cole had practiced the lie for so long and so well that he sometimes forgot that he was actually guilty.

Next, it was Veronica's turn to face the jury and present her case. She straightened her posture and approached the jury, her demeanor shifting from attorney to advocate. "Ladies and gentlemen," she began, her tone warm yet firm, "you have heard a compelling narrative from the prosecution. But I urge you to remember that a narrative is not a fact; it is merely a story woven from selective details."

She gestured towards Cole, whose heart raced beneath the weight of her words and what hung in the balance. "Ethan Cole is an artist, a man whose life has been dedicated to storytelling. He has experienced loss and heartbreak, but he is not a murderer. He did not kill Calvin Reese. He loved his work, and despite the challenges he faced, he would never resort to violence as a means of revenge or for any other reason."

A murmur rippled through the courtroom, a flicker of dissent in the audience. Ethan could sense the jury's interest shifting as his lawyer continued.

"The prosecution has painted a picture of motive, but I challenge you to look beyond that. We will provide evidence that shows Ethan's whereabouts during critical moments and testimony from those who know him best. You will hear from friends, family, and colleagues—people who can attest to his character. We will show you that there are others with far more reason to kill Calvin Reese."

Pierce turned her gaze to the jury, her expression earnest. "In this courtroom, we seek the truth. I implore you not to let the emotional weight of the prosecution's claims cloud your judgment. The burden of proof lies with them, and I assure you, they will not meet that burden."

As she stepped back, Ethan felt a flicker of hope ignite within him. Maybe, just maybe, they could turn this around.

The next witness called to the stand on behalf of the prosecution was Margot Lanes, her demeanor a mix of apprehension and resolve as she took her place in front of the jury. The prosecution began their questioning, emphasizing her relationship with Reese and the animosity that had bubbled beneath the surface after his reviews.

"Ms. Lanes," DA Kline began, his tone almost cordial, "how would you describe your relationship with Calvin Reese?"

Margot hesitated, her eyes darting to Ethan before focusing on Kline. "It was complicated. He was a powerful voice in the industry, and while I admired his work, I often disagreed with his critiques. His words could make or break an author's career."

"Did you feel that Mr. Cole was justified in his anger towards Reese?" Kline pressed, his eyes narrowing.

Margot shifted uncomfortably. "I think anyone would feel angry after being publicly humiliated, but that doesn't mean they'd resort to murder."

"Thank you, Ms. Lanes," Kline said, a hint of satisfaction in his tone. He turned to the jury, raising an eyebrow. "So, you believe Mr. Cole had reason to be upset, yet you do not believe he would kill?"

"I believe he's capable of anger, but not necessarily murder," Margot replied, her voice steady.

As Kline continued to question her, Ethan's thoughts raced. Margot had defended him, but how far would that defense hold? He could sense the scales tipping, and he knew they had to strike back hard.

After a lengthy cross-examination, Veronica eventually took her turn. "Margot, you've mentioned that you and Mr. Reese had a complicated relationship. Would you say he had any enemies in the literary community?"

Margot hesitated, a flicker of hesitation crossing her face. "He had critics, certainly. People who disagreed with him vehemently."

Veronica pressed further. "Can you name anyone who might have had a strong motive to harm him?"

Margot's gaze shifted, and Cole could see the gears turning in her mind. "There was Jillian Hargrove. She was furious about a review he wrote, and it affected her career significantly."

The courtroom erupted in whispers, and Cole felt a wave of relief wash over him. "Yes! That's it," he thought. "If they could draw attention to Jillian, it could divert suspicion away from him."

As Margot continued to talk about the connections within the literary community, Ethan felt a new sense of determination rising within him. They had a chance to unearth the truth and expose the killer. The walls around him seemed to soften.

The courtroom buzzed like an overcrowded hive, the sharp scent of tension mixing with the faint aroma of old wood polish. Veronica Pierce, lead defense attorney and rising star in the city's most prestigious law firm, sat at the defense table with her client, Ethan Cole. She adjusted the silk scarf at her neck, a small but calculated move to mask her nerves. The trial had only begun that morning, but the weight of the case was already pressing down on her.

Across the courtroom, the prosecutor's table gleamed with confidence. Assistant District Attorney David Kline, her longtime rival, shuffled his papers with an air of smug certainty. He had every reason to be confident. The case seemed airtight: Ethan Cole, the celebrated but controversial author, was accused of murdering Calvin Reese, a prominent book reviewer who had shredded Cole's latest novel in a scathing reviewer that went viral just weeks before his death. It was classic Reese.

Veronica cast a sidelong glance at Ethan, who sat impossibly calm beside her. Dressed in a dark suit that fit too well to be accidental, his demeanor was maddeningly self-assured for a man whose life hung in the balance.

"Is that the look you always wear in court?" he asked suddenly, his voice low but laced with flirtatious humor.

She blinked at him. "Excuse me?"

"That mix of fierce and... beautiful," he said, leaning in just enough for his words to reach her without being overheard. "It's distracting, is all. Like your perfume!" He was an expert-level flirt.

Veronica stiffened, her professional mask slipping for just a moment. She had dealt with charming defendants before, but Ethan was different. His gaze wasn't the leering kind she'd learned to deflect; it was penetrating, as if he were reading her feelings like one of his novels.

"Focus on your case, Mr. Cole," she said, her voice cool but not quite cold.

His lips quirked into a faint smile. "I'll try, but no promises." To which she smiled.

After a short recess the Judge banged his gavel and called the court back into session.

"Let's get underway here," he said.

As the opening arguments began, Veronica forced herself to focus on the facts: Calvin Reese had been found dead on the floor of his favorite cafe of unknown causes. Reese's bitter review of Ethan's first novel back in Grad School had accused the author of being "talentless, egotistical, and obsessed with violence," among other choice words. The long standing feud was fairly well known in the local literary community. It wasn't looking good for Cole.

That evening, Veronica paced her office, surrounded by piles of case files and a nearly empty bottle of Cabernet Sauvignon. She'd been Ethan's attorney for three weeks, and during that time, she'd come to understand two things: one, the evidence against him was both damning and circumstantial, and two, he was the most frustratingly compelling client she'd ever represented. She found herself firting with him and indulging in fantasies which was uncharacteristic for her.

The first time they'd met, she'd been struck by his presence. Ethan Cole wasn't conventionally handsome—his features were sharp, his jawline more severe than chiseled—but there was a quiet magnetism to him that made him hard to ignore. He had a way of speaking that felt like he was pulling you into a private world, his words carefully chosen, deliberate, almost intimate. She hated that she'd been thinking about him and outside the case.

Her phone buzzed, breaking her train of thought. A text from Ethan.

"Still pacing? Or are you finally letting yourself sit down?" he wrote.

She scowled, though she wasn't sure if it was at the message or at the fact that he'd somehow known what she was doing.

"You should be focusing on your testimony for the trial," she replied.

The reply came almost instantly. "I am. You're my best chance, remember?" He wrote.

Veronica sighed and tossed the phone onto her desk. Ethan was impossible. She reminded herself, not for the first time, that her job was to defend him, not to decipher him or allow him to romance her.

And yet, she couldn't shake the feeling that there was more to him than he let on. He had denied the murder from the start, claiming he hadn't even seen Calvin Reese in weeks. But his alibi was thin, his fingerprints, which were on file from being a Journalist in the Army, on various items like the

poison bottle, a wine glass and other items were impossible to explain away. His apparent lack of concern about the trial unnerved her. Was it because he was innocent or just trying to me cute? Or was it because, as a sociopath, he thought he could charm his way out of anything?

The next day, Ethan Cole took the stand. It was an unusual move for a defense case, but Veronica had decided it was their best shot. If anyone could cast doubt on the prosecution's narrative, it was Cole himself.

He looked unflappable as he answered Kline's questions, his voice steady and unhurried. When the Prosecutor pressed him about the fingerprints Cole tilted his head, as if amused by the question.

"I can't explain the fingerprints," he said, "because I didn't put them there. And lifting a finger print from a photograph, which the police tried to do, is unheard of. All I can tell you for sure is that I didn't kill Calvin Reese," Cole asserted.

"And yet you had every motive to do so," Kline said, his tone dripping with disdain. "Mr. Reese's review didn't just criticize your work—it humiliated you. It damaged your reputation and livelihood."

"Calvin's review didn't humiliate me," Ethan said, his voice cool. "It infuriated me, sure. But humiliation? That's a stretch. Writers grow thick skin, Mr. Kline. Comes with the territory."

Kline smirked. "So you expect this court to believe that you, an author known for writing violent revenge thrillers, didn't harbor any personal animosity toward reviewer Calvin Reese?"

Cole met his gaze without flinching. "I expect this court to believe the truth."

When Pierce rose for the defense cross-examination, she felt Cole's eyes on her as she approached the stand. She asked the questions she'd prepared, guiding him through his answers with precision, but there was a moment—just a moment—when she caught a flicker of something in his expression. Admiration? Amusement? She wasn't sure.

That night, Veronica found herself alone with Ethan in a conference room, reviewing the day's proceedings. The courthouse was nearly empty, the faint hum of fluorescent lights the only sound. "You handled yourself well on the stand today," she said, closing her notebook.

"Thanks to your guidance," he replied.

She looked up, surprised to find him watching her. The air between them felt charged, as if the trial itself had receded into the background, leaving only the two of them.

"You don't seem scared," she said after a moment.

"Should I be?" he asked.

"You're on trial for murder, Ethan. Most people would be terrified," she responded.

He smiled, "Most people haven't met you tho."

She opened her mouth to respond, but the words caught in her throat. She was a professional, dammit. She wasn't supposed to let herself be drawn in by a client, especially not one who might very well be guilty and headed for Death Row.

And yet, as Ethan leaned forward, his gaze locking with hers, she felt her resolve faltering. "Tell me something, Veronica," he said, his voice low. "Do you think I did it?"

She hesitated, her heart pounding. "It doesn't matter what I think. My job is to defend you."

"That's not what I asked," he said.

She held his gaze, the tension between them thick and undeniable. "I don't know," she admitted.

Cole leaned back, his smile enigmatic. "That's Fair enough. Maybe we could find out together?"

As he stood to leave, Veronica couldn't shake the feeling that Ethan Cole was hiding something. Whether it was a dangerous truth about Calvin Reese's murder or something far more innocuous, she didn't know.

All she knew was that she was drawn to him in a way she couldn't explain—and that her growing fondness of him terrified her more than any courtroom battle ever had.

As the courtroom settled in for another day of testimony, Ethan Cole again took his place on the witness stand, feeling the weight of countless eyes upon him. His pulse quickened as David Kline, the prosecution's sharp-eyed attorney, rose from his seat, an air of determination radiating from him. Ethan knew this moment was pivotal, a chance to express his feelings about critics, the very people whose words had spiraled him into this nightmare.

Kline approached with deliberate steps, a calculated smile on his face. "Mr. Cole," he began, his tone deceptively smooth, "I'd like to talk about your relationship with reviews and reviewers. How do you feel about critics in general?"

Cole squared his shoulders, the tension palpable in the room. "Critics?" he echoed, a bitter edge creeping into his voice. "They wield an incredible amount of power, and most of them don't even realize it. They sit in their ivory towers, armed with a keyboard, and take shots at the work of others without truly understanding the effort and emotion that goes into it. Most of them do not know what it's like to write a book."

Kline's brow raised slightly, his eyes glinting with interest. "So, you would say you have a particular disdain for critics?"

"Disdain? That's an understatement," Cole replied, his voice rising with passion. "They think their opinions are gospel. One review can ruin a writer's career overnight. It's like they have a license to kill —except they do it with words instead of weapons."

"Interesting choice of words, Mr. Cole," Kline noted, a sly grin spreading across his face. "You describe it as a kind of murder. Can you elaborate on why you would use that metaphor?"

Cole leaned forward, gripping the edge of the witness stand, his frustration boiling beneath the surface. "Because it feels like a murder! They assassinate not just the work but the very spirit of the artist. They tear apart the soul of the story, reducing it to mere words on a page. When Calvin Reese published his review, he didn't just critique my book—he took a shot at my entire career, my life's work. It was personal! Even back in Grad School he was jealous of my talent," Cole asserted.

Kline stepped closer, a hint of malice in his voice. "So, when you say it was personal, you mean to imply that the review had consequences beyond just your professional reputation?"

Ethan glared at him, his anger surging. "You don't get it, do you? These reviews just hurt the bottom line they can lead to self-doubt, to despair. I put everything into my writing, and when someone like Reese comes along and destroys it with a few

careless lines, it feels like they've stolen a part of me," he said.

Kline smirked, clearly enjoying the exchange. "And yet, despite this intense feeling, you still chose to write a book titled 'Death from Within', which suggests a preoccupation with violence and death. Doesn't that raise questions about your state of mind, particularly when faced with criticism?"

"Of course I chose that title!" Ethan shot back, his voice rising. "It was a metaphorical exploration, a reflection of the characters' internal struggles. It has nothing to do with real-life violence. And isn't it interesting that Mr. Reese basically copied the premise of my book and even made a similar book cover. A complete rip off!" His mask of sanity was slipping with rage coming to the forefront.

"Really?" Kline pressed, leaning in, his voice lowering conspiratorially. "Tell me, how did that make you feel?" The courtroom waited on an answer for what seemed like minutes.

"Angry? Sure. But not angry enough to…" Cole said his voice trailing off.

"Then when you wrote about a character poisoning someone in one of your novels, was that merely a figment of your imagination, or did it reflect a darker truth within you?" the DA asked.

Cole's eyes narrowed. "I'm a writer! I create stories, and sometimes those stories involve dark themes. It doesn't mean I condone them in real life. Writers use their craft to explore human nature—not to act out violent fantasies," he said.

"Yet you admit to harboring strong feelings against reviewers like Reese," Kline countered, his tone insinuating. "Would you say that anger could drive someone to commit… an irreversible act?"

"Stop twisting my words!" Cole barked, his frustration spilling over. "I'm not a killer! I'm a storyteller. My anger towards critics doesn't mean I would ever harm someone. It's a creative expression of frustration, not an actual desire to kill!"

Kline paused, letting the silence hang heavy in the air, then pressed on. "But your frustration was indeed palpable, Mr. Cole wasn't it? After all, it was this very frustration that led you to poison the pages of your book—a crime that has left a community in shock?" he said.

"Those are your words, not mine," Cole retorted, his voice strained but resolute. "My hatred for reviewers stems from their power to destroy dreams, not from any intention to kill. If you think that I would actually carry out something like that, you're completely mistaken."

The tension in the courtroom was palatable, the jury shifting in their seats, weighing Cole's passionate defense against Kline's relentless scrutiny. He could feel the stakes rising with every exchange, the implications of his words echoing long after the conversation had ended. This wasn't just a trial for his freedom; it was a battle for his very identity, a struggle to reclaim his narrative from the shadows that loomed over him.

As the trial continued, the atmosphere in the courtroom became increasingly charged. Ethan Cole felt the weight of the evidence against him pressing down like a future that was unavoidable as it would be unpleasant. Despite his determination to assert his innocence, he sensed the walls closing in as the DA's relentless questioning grew sharper.

It was another day on the stand, and Cole was feeling the strain. The prosecution had brought in expert witnesses to dissect the poison and its origin, linking it to Ethan's research. Yet, the real danger lay in the cross-examination, where DA Kline could exploit even the smallest crack in Ethan's testimony.

"Good Morning Mr. Cole," Kline began, his voice smooth and cutting like glass, "you stated yesterday that you felt deeply hurt and betrayed by Calvin Reese's review. Would you agree that such emotions can sometimes lead to irrational actions?"

Cole, was again feeling a surge of frustration, answering, "I was hurt, yes, but that doesn't mean I would act on those feelings. Writers get criticized all the time; it's part of the job. You deal with it."

"Is that so?" Kline replied, a calculating gleam in his eye. "Let's talk about 'Death on the Page'. In that book, you explored the theme of betrayal—specifically, how it can drive someone to desperate actions, correct?"

"Ahhhhh so you did read it then!?" Cole said with grin that got the courtroom laughing.

"Common Mr. Kline that is pure fiction!" Cole explained, trying to regain control. "It's not a reflection of my own feelings or actions."

Kline smiled, clearly enjoying the dance. "But you must admit, the line between fiction and reality can sometimes blur. Wouldn't you agree that your book character's motivations were sometimes shaped by intense emotions—like rage and resentment?"

Cole took a deep breath, trying to steady himself. "Characters are complex. They often reflect various aspects of human nature, but they don't dictate my actions. I can separate fiction from reality and a fact from a lie… Can you?"

DA Kline leaned in closer, his voice dropping conspiratorially. "Yet you do understand that sometimes, anger can manifest in real, irreversible ways, don't you? For instance, you've publicly expressed disdain for critics, which raises the question: What happens if anger goes unchecked?"

Cole felt the walls close in around him, the tension palpable. He replied, trying to remain calm, "Anger can be destructive, yes. But I would never let it get to the point of taking someone's life."

"Ah, but you see, Mr. Cole," Kline pressed, "this is where the story becomes murky. You said you'd never let that anger go unchecked. So, in a hypothetical situation, if you were pushed to your breaking point, you would agree that it's possible you could… lose control?"

Cole clenched his fists under the table, trying to maintain his composure. "That's not what I'm saying! I'm saying I'm capable of feeling strong emotions without acting on them."

Kline's eyes gleamed with the thrill of the hunt. "But you admit you felt strong emotions toward Reese. Would you describe them as extreme?"

Cole hesitated for a moment, feeling the pressure mounting. "It's hard to explain... I mean, I felt betrayed, and yes, it was extreme, but—"

"Extreme enough to consider a drastic action?" Kline interjected sharply, pressing his advantage. "Would you say you wanted to make him pay for the pain he caused you?"

A bead of sweat trickle down his forehead. "Wanted to make him pay?" Cole echoed, frustration boiling over. "No, I— You are putting words in my mouth!"

"Isn't it true that you thought about many ways to 'get back at him'?" Kline pressed. "That you contemplated how you could 'inflict pain on him' in response to his actions?" He condescendingly used his hands to indicate the quotation marks.

In that moment, the weight of Coles's emotions, the pressure of the courtroom, and the desire to defend himself collided in a chaotic whirlwind. "I just... wanted him to understand what his words could do! He deserved to feel the pain he caused me!" The words slipped out before he could catch them.

"So you killed him!" accused Kline.

"I didn't kill him," he protested. "But I wish I did!" He knew it was a mistake as soon as the words left his lips. The courtroom fell silent. Gasps echoed through the gallery, and Cole's heart sank as he realized the magnitude of his admission. Kline's eyes widened in triumph, a predatory smile creeping across his face.

"Understand what his words could do? You mean, you wanted him to suffer?" Kline's voice rang out, amplified by the silence in the room. "Is that not a direct admission of intent?" he asked to the whole courtroom without waiting or wanting an answer.

Cole's mind raced, panic flooding his senses as he tried to backtrack. "No! That's not what I meant! I was just trying to explain how hurtful his words were! I would never actually—"

But Kline cut him off, his voice dripping with satisfaction. "So you did consider the ramifications of his actions on your psyche. But what if your feelings led you down a darker path? A path where you might—"

"Objection!" Pierce shouted, rising from her seat. "This line of questioning is leading and suggestive. The defendant is not admitting to any crime!"

The judge's gavel came down with a resounding thud. "Sustained. Please rephrase your questions."

Ethan's heart pounded as he leaned back in his chair, breathless, the realization of his mistake hanging over him like a dark cloud. He had been so caught up in his defense, so blinded by the need to justify his feelings, that he had let slip the very thing that could seal his fate.

As Kline resumed his questioning, Cole felt a chill wash over him. The trial had shifted dramatically in that single moment, and now, the very words he had uttered would linger in the air, a haunting echo of his internal struggle—one that could lead to his ultimate undoing. He could do some serious time.

The trial continued to be a dance of narrative and counter-narrative, each side weaving their stories with the threads of evidence and testimony. The prosecution brought forth expert witnesses who dissected the poison found in Reese's system, and the forensic analysis that seemed to lead directly back to Ethan's workspace.

"Is it true, Mr. Cole," Kline asked during his cross-examination, "that you had recently been experimenting with a new recipe for a poison used in your writing. Why would you need to do that?"

Cole's heart sank as the DA unveiled a bottle holding it up for the jury to see. "The police found you had poisons didn't you?" he asked.

Cole swallowed hard, his mind racing. "It's a part of my research," he said, his voice steady. "I write fiction and I feel it's important to fully understand things. I've always incorporated elements of realism into my work. But that does not mean I would ever use it to harm anyone."

"And how do you test these poisons?" Kline asked.

"Objection!" Pierce yelled as she stood up. "My client is not a scientist or doctor and there's no proof he ever did anything with these substances."

"Overruled!" said the Judge banging the gavel.

The jury was silent, the gravity of his words hanging in the air. And he could see skepticism creeping into the expressions of the Jury and virtually everyone. The poison bottle was a potent symbol, one Kline wielded like a .45.

On cross examination Veronica was quick to respond, however. "Mr. Cole, can you explain why you felt it necessary to research and handle substance like that for your writings and books?"

Ethan leaned forward, his voice unwavering. "I wanted to create a narrative that was not only compelling but also grounded in reality. The characters in my book deal with conflict and consequences—this was merely an exploration of the human condition through fiction, not an admission of guilt. In one story I needed to know how one would create a poison and then write about that. Sometimes one must do to write realistically."

As the day wore on, Ethan felt the weight of scrutiny upon him. Each witness brought their own story, each piece of evidence was another blow against him. But as the prosecution's case began to face scrutiny and under the weight of their own inconsistencies, Cole's hope began to return. Eventually, the day came to a close, and the judge called for a recess. As the courtroom emptied, Ethan caught Veronica's eye. She offered him a slight nod, an unspoken promise that they would fight back.

Outside the courthouse, a throng of reporters, their cameras flashing like fireflies in the dusk pounced. "Ethan! Do you have a comment on today's proceedings?" a journalist shouted. Ethan pushed through the crowd, flanked by Veronica and Mills. "No comment!" he shouted back.

As they reached the safety of their car, he exhaled a long breath. The trial was underway, and while the stakes were higher than ever, Ethan Cole felt that at least he was no longer just a passive participant. And the best thing to him was getting to know and hit on his gorgeous attorney. He was fighting for his life, ready to challenge the narrative and reclaim his story and unveil the dark secrets of the literary world he once adored.

CHAPTER 11

Judgement Day
The Truth will Set you Free?

After almost 10 days of testimony from experts and witnesses, the case teased its conclusion. The courtroom buzzed with anticipation, a palpable tension filling the air as Ethan Cole sat at the defendant's table, his palms clammy against the smooth wood. The days of trial had blurred into a haze of relentless questioning, glaring evidence, and emotional turmoil. He had fought fiercely to maintain his feigned innocence, yet as he glanced at the jurors—faces solemn and unreadable—he felt the ground shift beneath him. The crushing weight of despair clawed at his insides, making it difficult to breathe. The reality of his guilt was rationalized as justified because of Reese's actions, not his own. To him Reese was an asshole who got what he deserved. And if he could get off on Murder, it would make a great book sure to be a best seller.

The no nonsense Judge entered the chamber, and it fell silent, all eyes drawn to the imposing figure in the black robe. The gavel struck, echoing like a death knell. "Court is now in session," the judge declared, his voice steady and authoritative. "We are here today to deliver the verdict in the case of the State versus Defendant Ethan Cole."

Cole's heart raced, pounding in his chest like a war drum. He had rehearsed every possible scenario in his mind, each one worse than the last. The haunting echo of his own words, twisted and turned by the prosecution, played on a loop in his thoughts. Despite his efforts, he felt the noose tightening with every moment spent on the stand and every hour in the courtroom. In the back of his mind he knew.

The judge looked directly at the jury. "Mr. Foreman, you have deliberated, and have you reached a verdict? Will you please stand?"

"We have your honor,' the foreman, a middle-aged man with glasses and a tweed jacket, said as he stood up.

"Please proceed," directed the Judge.

Glancing at Cole for just a moment before focusing on the judge, the Foreman continued, "Your Honor, we find the defendant, Ethan Cole..." there was a pause that felt like it was a year-long as everyone was silently waiting, "Guilty of Murder in the death of citizen Calvin Reese."

The words hung in the air like a heavy fog. Cole felt as if the ground had fallen away beneath him, leaving only an abyss, and everything seemed to morph into slow motion. His breath caught in his throat as he turned to look at Pierce, his attorney, whose face was a mask of shock and dismay. She had fought hard for him and had believed in his innocence, but now her spirit seemed crushed under the weight of the verdict. The entire defense team and the Cole supporters in the courtroom were in a state of shock. Other court watchers were not.

The judge continued the proceedings, his voice steady but devoid of any warmth. "In accordance with the laws of this state, I hereby sentence you, Ethan Cole, to life in prison with the possibility of parole. Bailiff? please take him into custody!"

The sentence struck him like a physical blow. A cold chill swept over him, freezing the world around him. Life in prison. The words echoed in his mind, a mantra of despair. Everything he had worked for, every word he had penned, had led to this moment —a moment that shattered his dreams.

"Court is now adjourned," the judge declared, his gavel coming down once more, sealing Cole's fate.

As the officers put him in handcuffs to escort him out, Ethan felt a sense of disbelief wash over him. He stood slowly, his legs unsteady as if they could barely support the weight of his despair. He really believed he would get away with it.

The courtroom began to empty, the murmurs of the spectators fading into the background as he was led away. His mind raced with thoughts of what could have been, of all the stories left untold, of the life he had imagined before the darkness crept in. He had never wanted this, never wished to see the inside of a prison cell, yet here he was, trapped in a nightmare of his own making. His story did not persuade.

As he walked through the corridor, flanked by guards, the reality of his situation sunk in. His books, once celebrated and cherished, would now be overshadowed by the shadow of murder. He had become the monster he had always written about, an outcast in his own life.

"Ethan!" a voice called out, breaking through the haze of despair. He turned slightly to see Veronica pushing through the crowd of onlookers, her tear-stained face drawn and pale. "Ethan, I'm sooooo sorry. I fought as hard as I could—"

"Save it," he interrupted the bitterness in his voice sharper than he intended. "You did your best, but it just wasn't enough. I let my emotions get the better of me, and now look where it's gotten me."

She reached for his arm, but he stepped back, unwilling to feel comfort in the face of his ruin. "I should have been stronger, more composed. I can't believe they found me guilty."

"Ethan, they twisted your words. We'll appeal this," she insisted, desperation creeping into her voice.

He shook his head, a hollow laugh escaping his lips. "An appeal? For what and with what money? To go through this charade again? No, it's done. They've made their decision," Cole said coldly. The guards led him toward the prisoner exit door, each step feeling heavier than the last. He glanced back one final time, meeting Veronica's eyes filled with a mix of compassion and frustration. "I'll be fine," he said, though he knew it was a lie.

The door swung open, and the harsh light of the outside world flooded in, a stark contrast to the shadows of the courtroom. As Ethan was ushered through, he felt the weight of his reality crashing down around him. He was going to prison—not just for the crime committed, but for the man he was.

In the wake of his own destruction and in his heart of hearts he knew he deserved what was coming. Outside the courtroom, reporters clamored for comments, cameras flashing like fireflies in the dimming light of the day. "Ethan! Any comment on

the verdict?" one shouted, but Cole's heart was too heavy to respond. He felt as if he were walking through a storm, each question, each flash of light hitting him like raindrops from a dark sky.

"Get me outta here," he muttered to the guard, feeling an overwhelming urge to escape the media chaos.

The guard nodded, leading him through a side door and into the sterile corridors of the jail, the walls closing in as he moved farther away from the courtroom—and the world he once knew. The metallic clang of cell doors reverberated in his ears, a grim reminder of the fate that awaited him.

Inside the holding area, he was stripped of his belongings, each item a piece of his identity: his belt, his watch, his very clothes—signifiers of a life that felt increasingly foreign. The officer's hands moved swiftly, efficiently, as if they were accustomed to processing souls like his. Perhaps the most devastating and debilitating was when the

Guard forced him to give up his writers notebook from his back pocket.

"Turn around," the officer commanded, and Ethan complied, feeling the coldness of the room seep into his bones. The click of handcuffs echoed in the silence, a sound that marked the beginning of his incarceration. He had read about this in the stories he loved to tell—about men broken by confinement, stripped of their dreams and ambitions. But now it was Fact not fiction and he was one of his book characters trapped in his own tragic narrative.

The next morning, after a sleepless night in county jail, he was transferred to the state prison in legging chain and handcuffs. As he was led to his cell, the reality of his surroundings hit him. He was a Murderer. Welcome to Cell 149! The small, cramped space was painted a dull puke green, the flickering fluorescent light casting eerie shadows across the concrete walls. A narrow bed, a sink, and a toilet made up the entirety of his new home. The air felt stale and oppressive, filled with the scent of despair. The sounds of men behind bars filled the air; yelling, barked orders from guards, arguments, toilets flushing... the sounds of life behind bars.

As Cole, now Prisoner #43187, stepped inside his new home, the heavy metal door clanging shut behind him with doom. The sound reverberated in his ears, a finality that felt like a guillotine's blade poised to fall. He sank onto the edge of the bed, staring at the blank wall in front of him, fighting against the suffocating despair that threatened to engulf him. He began to cry.

In the darkness of his thoughts, he replayed the trial the moment he had slipped up and admitted to wanting Reese to feel the pain he had inflicted. How had it come to this? He truly thought that he could and would get away with it all. Now he was a writer brought low by his own words, entangled by a web of emotion and regret.

Hours turned into days, and the reality of prison life began to settle in. The rhythm of prison, with its clanging doors, shouting inmates, and distant cries, formed a haunting symphony that accompanied his every waking moment. Ethan tried to hold on to the fragments of his identity, but each day felt like a slow erosion of self, a steady encroachment of hopelessness. Prison was designed to do that.

He had become a ghost in his own story, a man whose words no longer mattered. Each thought of his books, the characters he had crafted with such care, faded into the background like whispers in the wind. He was now a mere number—one among many, lost in a system that cared little for stories.

Days turned into weeks that turned to months, and Ethan found himself in the prison library, seeking solace in the pages of long-forgotten novels. There other prisoners called him 'Worm' as in 'Bookworm'. He clung to the words of others, searching for a glimpse of hope in tales that spoke of redemption, of characters who overcame insurmountable odds. But even as he read, the realization gnawed at him: he had become the antagonist in his own life, a man trapped by his choices, suffocated by his anger. He was now a convicted killer and nothing would change that.

In the quiet moments of the night, when the world around him settled into a reluctant slumber, Cole often found himself reflecting on his past. He replayed every scene, every moment leading to Calvin Reese's death, wondering if there had been a single choice that could have altered his path. The haunting look Reese gave him as he lay on the floor of the cafe could not be erased from his memory. He often asked himself... What if he had simply ignored the review? What if he had channeled his pain into a story, rather than letting it consume him? But it was too late for "what ifs." The prison walls encased him like a tomb, the weight of his conviction hanging heavy on his shoulders. Each morning, he awoke to the same stark reality, the same reminder of his sentence. A life without freedom. A life devoid of the passion that had once fueled him. He had few visitors.

And yet, even in the depths of despair, a flicker of determination began to ignite within him. He refused to let this be the end of his story. He was still a writer, and the darkness would not define him. He would find a way to reclaim his voice, to transform his pain into something meaningful, even within the confines of a prison cell. If fate has seen fit to put him here he would make sure to publish somehow.

Having a pen and paper is a privilege for convicts in prison. As he picked up a pen, feeling the familiar weight of it in his hand, a surge of resolve washed over him. He could still write—could still breathe life into the characters that danced in his imagination. The ink would flow, and through it, he would reclaim his narrative, even if it meant doing so from behind bars.

Ethan began to write again, not just as a way to escape but as a means of confronting his reality. He filled pages with raw emotion, stories that mirrored his own struggles, his inner turmoil, and the pain of the reality of his real guilt. He poured his heart into each line, capturing the essence of what it felt like to be trapped and desperate, yet yearning for freedom.

His words became an outlet, a cathartic release. They spoke of love, loss, and redemption, weaving a tapestry of life that resonated with the truths he had buried deep within. The prison library became his sanctuary, a place where he could lose himself in the rhythm of his thoughts and the cadence of his pen. He wrote about the shadows of his past, about Calvin Reese, about the tempest of emotions that had led him down this path.

As weeks turned into months, Ethan found solace in his new routine. Each morning, he awoke with the dawn, determined to seize the day, even if it was

confined to the four walls of his cell. He would write until his hand ached, crafting stories that, while rooted in darkness, still glimmered with the possibility of light.

But the shadows of his conviction loomed large, and the outside world continued to spin on without him. He could see the fleeting glimpses of life beyond the prison walls through small windows that allowed the sun to seep in, illuminating the cold concrete of his surroundings. He could hear laughter, and sounds of life outside, taunting him with memories of what he had lost.

Over the years in prison therapy Cole discovered the importance of confronting one's past or at least recognizing it and being honest about what occurred to put you behind bars in the first place. And while it was one thing to admit guilt in court it was a whole different matter to admit to yourself the mistakes one has made. He'd always maintained his innocence to any and all but to truly move forward he now knew he had to admit what he had done and what had occurred to take his name and give him a number from the state.

The memories hit Ethan like a dull blade slipping between his ribs—cold, precise, and impossible to ignore. He closed his eyes and was back in his lab and at the cafe watching Reese.

The poison Cole chose for his plan wasn't easy to come by, nor was it something the average person had even heard of. Called 'Tetraxin', it was an exceptionally rare and highly controlled neurotoxin, the sort of compound known only to a select few in toxicology circles and the underworld of illegal laboratories. Its origins were murky, rumored to be an experimental toxin abandoned by the military and pharmaceutical companies for its unpredictability and terrifying potency. Cole had spent weeks in the darkest corners of the web, paying a small fortune to a contact who promised Tetraxin was as undetectable as it was deadly. To him, it was a perfect tool. It was similar to a poison used by the Russian KGB... Thallium. Deadlier than cyanide it is similar to Polonium-210 used to kill a Russian spy in 2006. It was only after a full autopsy and lab workup that it was discovered.

The toxin was nearly perfect for his needs. Tetraxin is colorless and odorless, a transparent phantom that would go unnoticed on a surface before invading the body. Ethan's method of delivery was meticulous:

he coated each page in a thin, invisible layer of Tetraxin, allowing it to soak in overnight and dry to a touch as smooth as untreated paper and virtually invisible. Handling the poison had required gloves, steady hands, and more courage than he had ever imagined needing. He had to test it. But how?

Cole went to the local pet store and purchased a lab rat. He placed the book with its open pages in the large aquarium and then released the rodent into it. After smelling it and inspecting it, the rat promptly ignored it and repeatedly walked across it and stopped to smell the pages. Cole's heart sank when it seemed the poison was having no effect. "Shit! This isn't gonna work." He thought to himself. "Maybe I should just shoot the son of a bitch!" After watching it for almost an hour, he went to sleep, leaving his test subject to the cage and the night. In the morning, the lab rat was dead, and Ethan Cole was a happy man.

After two passes with a Tetraxin coating of the cover and pages, Cole's book had become a silent weapon disguised as innocently as any bestseller. Once absorbed through the skin, Tetraxin worked in gradual, sinister stages, mirroring a natural flu-like illness. It was known for its stealthy progression: exposure began with subtle fatigue, an ache behind the eyes, easily mistaken for a passing headache. Within a day or two, the toxin would start attacking the nervous system, causing sporadic tingling in the fingertips and toes. The symptoms would then escalate in a horrifying but subtle chain, making the victim feel as though they were simply having a "bad spell." By the time the telltale signs of severe poisoning set in—spasms, severe vertigo, fever, and paralysis of the extremities and of breath—death was nearly inevitable.

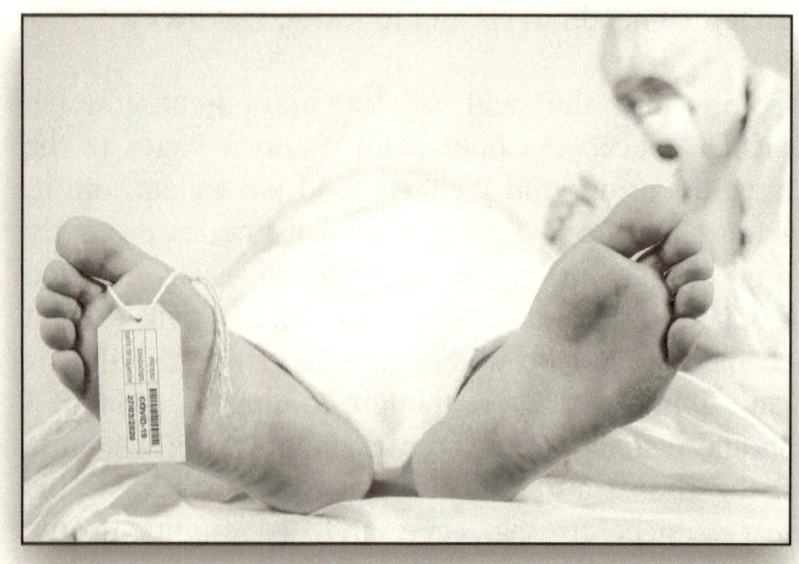

What made Tetraxin particularly lethal was its ability to mimic natural neurological deterioration. The toxin's slow, insidious attack on the central nervous system would baffle doctors, leading them down false diagnostic paths. For Calvin Reese, an older man with a high-stress job, doctors would likely suspect anything from severe migraines to heart issues or even a neurological disorder. The effects were not only lethal but also undetectable in standard autopsies, especially if small, continuous doses were applied over time. The poison's molecular structure broke down upon death, leaving only a faint residue, which would likely go unnoticed by all but the most meticulous forensic specialists. Come what may, in the way of intervention, the infected victim would be dead in a week. And unless authorities were actively looking for something, it would appear that the person had simply died of the flu.

Ethan had done his research and knew the poison would bind with natural oils on the skin, seeping in with each flip of a page. He had counted on Calvin's own habits as a critic: the way he would always flip through a book impatiently, flipping back to reread passages with disdain, thus allowing the poison to enter his bloodstream incrementally. In his mind, it was poetic justice—Reese's own compulsion to dissect and criticize every word would be the very mechanism of his death. Cole smiled at the thought.

His choice of delivery method was equally diabolical and almost as calculated as the poison itself. Rather than merely delivering a lethal dose in one sitting, he had crafted the experience to be a slow death, a death that would eat away at Reese day by day. The symptoms would align so closely with his life's stresses that he would never suspect a deliberate attack. To anyone observing him, the critic would simply look worn out, overworked, sick and maybe even paranoid—a downfall for a man devoted to hurting others with a pen.

In the final hours, Tetraxin would unleash its true horror. As Reese's body grew weaker and his mind began to suffer, the toxin would take full control. He would experience excruciating muscle spasms, a disorienting loss of balance, blindness and eventually, the paralysis that would halt his lungs and stop his heart. It was a protracted death that mirrored the kinds of endings Reese himself had derided Ethan for writing, a tragic irony that brought a cruel satisfaction to Ethan's mind.

Cole spent weeks perfecting the mixture, ensuring the poison was untraceable and slow enough to seem natural. Reese would feel nothing at first, just a vague discomfort—a whisper of something wrong. And before long, with any luck, it would be too late.

What made Tetraxin particularly lethal and hard to detect was its ability to mimic natural neurological deterioration. The toxin's slow, insidious attack on the central nervous system would baffle doctors, leading them down false diagnostic paths. For Calvin Reese, an out of shape older man with a high-stress job, doctors would likely suspect anything from severe migraines to heart issues, the flu or even a neurological disorder.

The effects were not only lethal but also undetectable in standard autopsies, especially if small, continuous doses were applied over time. The poison's molecular structure broke down upon death, leaving only a faint residue, which would likely go unnoticed by all but the most meticulous forensic specialists. Come what may, in the way of intervention, the infected victim would be dead in a week. And unless authorities were actively looking for something, it would appear that the person had

simply died of the flu. At the time he felt he was justified but now he knew it was wrong.

About six months later came a day when Ethan received an unexpected visitor—a letter from Veronica. His heart raced as he opened it, the familiar handwriting sending waves of nostalgia crashing over him.

"Dearest Ethan," it began, *"I hope this letter finds you well, or as well as can be expected under the circumstances. I've been thinking about you constantly, and I want you to know that I'm not*

giving up on you. There's so much more to your story, and I'm determined to help you find a way to prove your innocence and get you a new trial!"

He read her words over and over, absorbing the hope embedded in each sentence. She spoke of filing an appeal, of gathering evidence that had been overlooked during the trial. She encouraged him to keep writing, to harness his creativity and let it guide him through the darkness. *"You're more than just a friend to me and your voice matters to people,"* she wrote. *"It always has. Please don't give up hope...I know you didn't do this!"* He didn't have the heart to tell her the truth, Coward that he was he doubted he'd ever have the courage.

A swell of emotions coursed through Cole as he finished the letter. He had felt so isolated, so lost, and yet here was a lifeline, a flicker of hope and love that ignited a fire within him. He took a deep breath, feeling a renewed sense of purpose surge through him, and folded up the frayed letter. All he really wanted was to walk on a beach with her.

The following day, with a determination he hadn't felt in a long time, he wrote back to Veronica. He shared his experiences in prison, the stories he had begun to craft, and his desire to fight for his freedom. He outlined his plans for the future, detailing how he envisioned the appeal process unfolding, and how he would assist her.

"Together, I hope we can turn this around," he penned, feeling the weight of his words as they flowed onto the page. "I refuse to be defined by my mistakes. I 'll write the ending of my own story."

Days turned into weeks, and he sent his letters to Pierce with anticipation, waiting for her responses as if they were lifelines thrown into the turbulent prison waters. Her replies came often, filled with legal jargon, plans of action, encouragement and a hint of something more. The prospect of an appeal became a beacon of hope in his otherwise bleak reality. The idea that she could maybe fall in love with him was more than be could believe possible. But he thought it was not to be and that he would be in the service of the state for the rest of his life.

In prison his writing flourished, Cole began to use his incarceration to fuel his creativity. He envisioned a novel, a reflection of his journey, capturing the raw emotions of despair, anger, and ultimately, redemption. He would write about the complexities of human nature, about the dangers of letting one's emotions dictate actions, and the power of second chances. He immediately got busy.

With each passing day, he found himself immersed in his work, and the prison walls became less of a prison and more of a sanctuary where he could create. The guards and convicts began to notice his transformation, some even offering nods of respect as he was diligently writing in his cell.

Time slipped away like a million grains of sand through an hourglass, and before he knew it 10 years had passed. He had found a publisher and was working on a second novel he would release from prison. His first book 'Second Chances'; was nominated for a Pulitzer Prize. The state would keep 89% of all proceeds. Cole's writing became his lifeline. He poured his heart and soul into every story, determined to weave the truth of his experiences into something meaningful. He created characters that embodied his struggles, crafting narratives that spoke to the human condition, of love and loss, and the relentless pursuit of redemption. Human stories that would resonate with all readers.

Then, one fateful day, he received news that the appellate court had agreed to hear his case. A feeling of hope surged within him like an unquenchable flame, igniting a determination he had thought lost forever. Cole could almost taste freedom again, the sweet nectar of possibility tantalizing his senses.

As he prepared for the Appeal, he found himself reflecting on the journey that had brought him to this moment. The anger, the despair, the mistakes—each had shaped him, but they did not define him. He was still Ethan Cole, still a writer, and prison had armed him with some great stories to tell.

The day of the appeal finally arrived, and Cole stood in front of the judges, the weight of his past heavy on his shoulders but the glimmer of hope illuminating his path. He spoke passionately, not just about his rehabilitation but about the importance of narrative—the power of stories to shape lives, to heal wounds, and to provide understanding.

"I'm more than the mistakes I've made," he declared, his voice steady and resolute. "I am a writer, a storyteller, and I am innocent. I deserve the chance to reclaim my life. My story isn't over, and neither is my fight for justice," said Convict #43187. "I can make a positive contribution," he added.

As he finished speaking, he caught a glimpse of the members of the parole board their expressions were thoughtful, positive and engaged. Perhaps, just perhaps, they were beginning to see the man behind the crime. But it remained to be seen if his testimony and the trial irregularities that Pierce had ID'd would be enough for Cole to regain his freedom. The prison was also very overcrowded so some convicts were being released early 'for time served'. It was another possibility for freedom.

When the appeal verdict was finally delivered six weeks later, it felt as though time had stopped. Holding his breath Cole's heart raced in anticipation. The judges announced their decision to overturn his conviction, citing insufficient evidence, police over reach when they continued to question Cole after he expressly stated he wanted his lawyer and procedural errors during the trial. The wave of relief that washed over him was overwhelming, and he felt the shackles of despair begin to loosen.

With tears of joy streaming down his face, Cole realized that he had not only regained his freedom but had also gotten a second chance. He was no longer defined by his past; true he was a killer, but he was also a survivor, a storyteller ready to write the next chapter of his life and share captivating stories with the world.

As he stepped out of the courthouse, the sun shone brightly, illuminating the path ahead. The world felt vibrant and alive, filled with possibilities he had once thought lost forever. He had survived the storm, and now, he was ready to embrace the life he had fought so hard to reclaim.

With a renewed sense of purpose, Cole looked ahead, knowing that at age 53 his story was far from over. He would continue to create, write and tell the tales that needed to be told. He was now determined to fight for those who had lost their voices or had never had one. In the depths of despair, he had discovered his greatest strength: the power of storytelling and the unbreakable spirit of a writer determined to rise from the ashes of incarceration. He had found that God rewards misdeeds just usually not in the way we usually want.

CHAPTER 12

Reclamation
A Rehabilitated Killer?

Almost eleven years had passed and one-time award-winning Author Ethan Cole stepped out of the prison gates and into the warm afternoon sunshine. He was thinner now and grayer, the heavy metal door clanging shut behind him with a finality that reverberated in his chest. It was the first time in almost a decade that he could see the blue sky without barbed wire in the way! The sun bathed him in warmth, the rays breaking through the clouds like a promise of new beginnings. After so many long years behind bars, he was finally free—a phrase he had repeated to himself like a mantra during those interminable nights spent alone in his tiny institutional green cell.

The world beyond the prison walls buzzed with life, vibrant and chaotic. Cole took a deep breath, inhaling the scent of freshly cut grass and blooming flowers, sensations that felt foreign and intoxicating. The air was crisp and filled with the distant sounds of laughter, children playing, and cars passing by— remnants of the world he had left behind and the new life he yearned to reclaim. Now all he wanted was to walk on the beach in the moonlight preferably with Ms. Pierce by his side.

As he stepped forward, he felt the weight of his past

press against him, a familiar shroud that whispered the memories of anger, despair, and the consequences of allowing the opinions of others to dictate his emotions. He remembered the scathing reviews that had set him on this path—a mere opinion that had morphed into a catalyst for rage, leading him to make choices that had irrevocably altered the trajectory of his life. He had started to come to grips with his guilt but…

The past decade had been a relentless journey of introspection. In the confines of his cell, he had reflected on the fragility of human emotion and how easily anger could twist one's judgment. He had allowed a critic's words to seep into his soul, to fester and grow until they consumed him, transforming him into a man he barely recognized. It had taken losing everything—his freedom, his reputation, his very identity—for him to grasp the dangerous power of letting others' perceptions shape his reality. He knew he could never make killing Reese OK but he had paid his 'debt to society' and rationalized that he and karma were even.

"Ethan Cole!" a voice called out, jolting him from his reverie. A woman approached, her features striking and familiar. It was Veronica, her eyes shimmering with unshed tears. She was gorgeous and rushed forward, embracing him tightly as if she was afraid he would vanish again. They kissed for only the second time and it was long and tender. They stood outside the gate in the sun for awhile.

"I can't believe you're finally out!" she said.

"Me neither," he replied, his voice thick with emotion. "It all feels surreal."

As they pulled apart, Cole took a moment to study her. The years had etched new lines on her face, but her spirit still unbroken and she was still a babe.

"Thank you, thank you, thank you! You fought for me, didn't you?" he asked with gratitude.

"Always! Every step of the way," she affirmed, her smile warm and genuine. "And I'm so proud of you. I've missed you. You've come back to us, Ethan."

"Not entirely," he admitted, a shadow flickering across his expression. "I'm still grappling with the echoes of the past. It's hard not to feel the weight of those years. But we'll get there," he said.

Veronica nodded knowingly, her gaze compassionate. It was not lost on her that he had used the word 'we'. "It's natural to carry that burden but remember what you've learned. You've transformed that mistake into something beautiful through your writing and books. Don't let the opinions of others hold you hostage ever again."

"Words are powerful things," Cole mused, his voice reflective. "They can uplift or destroy. I let one person's opinion cloud my judgment, and it cost me everything. It's a lesson I won't soon forget."

"Exactly," she replied, her enthusiasm rekindled as she flipped her long blond hair. "You have a chance to share that lesson now. Your story, your journey—it can help others understand the danger of letting rage and bitterness take control."

Cole's heart raced as the enormity of her words sank in. He had been given a second chance, a rare opportunity to use his experiences to guide others. "You're right," he said, a spark igniting within him. "If I can help even one other person avoid the mistakes I made, it'll all be worth it."

With a newfound determination, Ethan turned to face his new horizon. He would reclaim his narrative —not just as a writer but as a man shaped by effort and understanding. He envisioned a world where stories could bridge divides and where emotions could be articulated without the fear of judgment. Veronica Pierce, still single and now in her 40s, gestured toward the bustling street ahead.

"Let's go. There's so much to see, and you have a great life to live. I'd love to help you live it, " she said, clearly making a pass. He was flattered, and years behind bars, he was more than ready.

As they walked to her car together, Cole felt the thrill of possibility surge through him. Each step was a testament to his future, a reminder that he could be more than just a man defined by the mistakes of his past. He was a survivor and an artist with a story to tell built upon his mistakes and vision for the future.

The sun projected its golden hue over the landscape. Cole's heart swelled with hope and anticipation, the shadows of his previous life receding with every step he took. He resolved to face the world with open arms, ready to embrace the beauty of life, the connections that mattered, and the lessons he had learned the hard way.

As they ventured into the vibrant city, he contemplated the power of words. He knew the journey ahead would be filled with challenges, but armed with the wisdom of his experiences, he was prepared to meet them head-on.

But as he began to reflect during his time in prison, he started to understand that this cycle of hatred only perpetuated the very environment he despised. He came to realize that while reviewers might not be creators in the same sense, their voices still had the power to influence and shape narratives—just as Cole had the power to choose how to respond to them. The bitterness he felt was a chain that bound him, and it was time to break free.

Cole began to see that true strength lay not in responding to venom with venom but in rising above the noise, using the criticism as fuel to create something even more profound. His journey toward understanding the value of diverse voices, even those he once labeled as leeches, marked the first step toward reclaiming his narrative—not just as a writer, but as a man ready to embrace his craft. Prison had cost him more than a decade and had taken its toll...in the coming months Pierce would find that he talked a lot less and drank a lot more.

The danger of allowing others' opinions to shape his emotions had cost him dearly, but it had also gifted him the insight and, through years of therapy while incarcerated, the ability to rise above it all. The lesson was clear: rage could blind, anger can destroy but understanding and compassion had the power to heal. As he got ready to step back into the world, he vowed to wield his words with more care, to honor the stories that needed to be told, and to inspire others to reclaim their narratives and move beyond their mistakes. He knew he was a killer but in his mind he was a 'Nice guy.' Now he knew that in life one makes choices but living with them is an entirely other matter. He was sorry. In the end he came to understand that Reese and his idiotic opinions didn't deserve the fate he had dealt him.

The years behind bars forced Cole to come too grips with his past with brutal honesty. It is amazing what the human mind can erase. Through therapy and self examination he came to grips with his past, not that he wanted to be totally honest for fear of additional time in prison. His participation in his estranged wife's disappearance and in the killing of a local journalist who'd been writing a profile on him in almost the same way as his latest crime novel... it all came to the forefront. And at least to himself he confronted his guilt. 'I did it' he finally admitted, 'I am a killer.' There was no longer any rationalization for his actions. He'd come to terms with the terrible things he had done and was ready to move on. He wanted to be a productive member of the community and spread the idea of dealing with rage and hate before it gets out of hand and destroys.

With every heartbeat and step towards the prison gates, he felt more alive, more determined to carve out a place for himself in this new chapter of life. 'I am free!' he said to himself over and over. No longer would he allow the darkness of the past to define him. Author Ethan Cole is ready to embrace his new life and a new love. Now he'd be all set if he could figure out how to tell his new love Veronica Pierce the truth, the whole truth and nothing but the truth!

 # Goodreads Author

★★★★★

"Awesome! It was like I was there at the battle. A GREAT read."
-Reader Review

Now Available

- Book
- eBook

Coming Soon!
- Audiobook
On Audible

www.authortommcauliffe.com

- Kindle
- Apple
- BaM
- Barns & Noble
- Amazon
- Smash words

★★★★★

Wow, I read this book all the way through. I could not put it down. It is that good!
-Amazon Review

<u>Acknowledgments</u>

Florida Bureau of Investigations

FBI Public Affairs Dept.

University of Florida
Dept. of Tropical Medicine

The Harvill Foundation

Cover Art by Mike & Tina Andaya
www.s7ms.com

The Team at Draft 2 Digital

Prof. Dale L Roberts

Editor Lisa Clute

Book Dragon Proofing

<u>Please Leave a Review!</u>

A Small Ask...

Now that you've finished reading this book, what do you think of what you read? Are there any tips or information you found insightful? What do you think is missing from this book? While you're thinking back on what you read, it'd mean the world to me if you left an honest review on Amazon and/or Goodreads.

As you probably know, reviews play a part in building relevancy for all products online. Whether you found the information enjoyable or worthless, your candid review helps others make an informed purchase.
Also, based on your review, I'll adjust this publication and future editions.

I appreciate your support!

Please send questions to:
Bookinfo@nextstopparadise.com

Member:

Alliance of Independent Authors

Emerald Coast Writers

Military Photojournalists Association

Florida Writers Association

Alliance of Independent Authors

Books by Author Tom McAuliffe

- Mr. Mulligan - *The Life of Champion Armless Golfer Tommy McAuliffe*

- Nuts! - *The Life & Times of Gen. Tony McAuliffe*

- Throttle Up - *Astronaut Teacher Christa McAuliffe*

- Mad Dog! - *Detroit Tiger Dick McAuliffe*

- Charmed - *From Motown to Combat & Back*

- Almost - *The Road to the Grande*

- Thunder Road - *Goodyear, God & Gatorade*

- Buddy, Brian and Me - *A Spooky Rock Story*

- Frozen - A W*WII and Mind over Matter Tale*

- Soft Shell - *Teddy the Talking Turtle*

- Max and Me - *Paws Across The Water*

- Off the Rock - *Escaping Alcatraz*

- Deepwater Oil - *Drillin on the Moon*

- Who Won? - *The 2024 Presidential Election*

- No Place Like Home - *The No BS RE Guide*

- The Lake - *Divided Waters*

- Death on the Page - *Revenge on the Reviewer*

Books - eBooks - Audio Books
Available at Amazon, Kindle and your fave book outlet

Also Available at:
WWW.AUTHORTOMMCAULIFFE.COM

MAX AND ME
A Story of Hope
YA
Tom McAuliffe

From the Award Winning Author of 'Mr. Mulligan'
OFF THE ROCK
Escaping Alcatraz
Tom McAuliffe

From the Award Winning Author of 'Mr. Mulligan'
Volume 4: The McAuliffe Series
Detroit Tiger
Dick McAuliffe
MAD DOG
TOM MCAULIFFE

Buddy
Brian and Me
Star Bar
Tom McAuliffe

Soft Shell
Teddy the Talking Turtle
YA
Tom McAuliffe

ALMOST
The Road to the Grande
Detroit Bands of the mid-to-late 60's...
You Almost Remember!
TOM MCAULIFFE

THUNDER ROAD
Goodyear, God & Gatorade!
TOM McAuliffe

FROM THE AWARD WINNING AUTHOR OF 'MR. MULLIGAN'
NUMBER 3 IN 'THE MCAULIFFE SERIES'
TEACHER ASTRONAUT
CHRISTA MCAULIFFE
THROTTLE UP!
TOM MCAULIFFE

Mr. Mulligan
Sometimes
Life is a
Do Over!
The Life of Champion Armless Golfer
Tommy McAuliffe
TRUE STORY
TOM McAULIFFE

FROZEN
A WWII Mind Over Matter Tale
Tom McAuliffe
From the Award Winning Author of 'Mr. Mulligan'

From the Award Winning Author of 'Mr. Mulligan'
No Place Like Home
The No BS Guide to Real Estate
•Buying •Selling •Investing
Realtor
TOM McAULIFFE

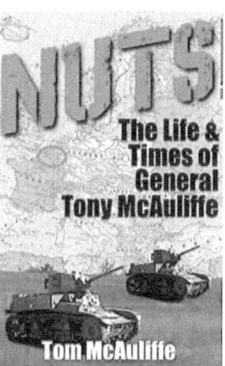

NUTS!
The Life & Times of General Tony McAuliffe
Tom McAuliffe

written by humans
not by AI